ROBERT J. KLEBERG PUBLIC LIBRARY
4th & Henrietta
Kingsville, Texas 78363
(512) 592-6381

1. Books may be kept two weeks, except 7 day books, and may be renewed once for the same period.
   No telephone renewals.
2. A fine is charged for each day a book is not returned according to the above rule. No book will be issued to any person incurring such a fine until it has been paid.
3. All injuries to books beyond reasonable wear and all losses shall be made good to the satisfaction of the Librarian.
4. Each borrower is held responsible for all books charged on his card and for all fines accruing on the same.
5. A Library card must be presented each time loans are made.

THE SCHOOL
OF DARKNESS

By Manly Wade Wellman

THE VOICE OF THE MOUNTAIN
WHAT DREAMS MAY COME
THE HANGING STONES
THE LOST AND THE LURKING
AFTER DARK
THE OLD GODS WAKEN

THE SCHOOL OF DARKNESS

MANLY WADE WELLMAN

DOUBLEDAY & COMPANY, INC.
GARDEN CITY, NEW YORK
1985

SF
Wel
m
copy 1

All of the characters in this book
are fictitious and any resemblance
to actual persons, living or dead,
is purely coincidental.

Library of Congress Cataloging in Publication Data

Wellman, Manly Wade, 1905–
　The school of darkness.

　I. Title.
PS3545.E52858S3　1985　　813'.54
　　　　ISBN: 0-385-19065-4
Library of Congress Catalog Card Number 85-12914

Copyright © 1985 by Manly Wade Wellman
First Edition
All Rights Reserved
Printed in the United States of America

In grateful memory of
Dorothy McIlwraith
and
Lamont Buchanan,
who were there the first time John Thunstone walked in

And in the School of Darkness learn
What mean
The things unseen
—John Banister Tabb

FOREWORD

Diligent inquiry goes to show that no real college or university called Buford exists in the United States. The campus and community here described resemble actual campuses and communities only in a general fashion. Characters and events are imaginary and are not based on real characters and events, although I dare hope that they seem real.

Manly Wade Wellman
Chapel Hill, North Carolina, 1984

THE SCHOOL
OF DARKNESS

I

That authoritative voice from somewhere or everywhere had commanded a fastening of seat belts, a cessation of smoking. The great plane tilted forward and lost altitude, tilted forward again so that the earth far below the porthole lost its maplike pattern, began to become living earth. Little fluffs of mossy green grew into distant clumps of trees; winking jewels became miniature ponds. There were slate streaks of highways, wee toys of barns and houses. The voice proclaimed that they were coming in to Sidney-Exeter Airport, were arriving on time.

The throbbing roar of the motors abated. A powerful banking turn, so that the horizon vanished from view at the porthole, and for moments nothing but sky showed there, blue as only April's sky can be, with tags of white cloud like shredded cotton. The great turn accomplished, downward again and earth rushing up, swiftly, threateningly, almost like a flood. And a sense of hanging helplessness. The plane was in the hands only of its pilot, Captain Somebody, wise and skilled, who in his time must have made thousands of safe, successful landings.

Then, close below there, the immense paved outstretch of the runway. And closer, down almost upon it, with a great fence rushing rearward there to the side. At last, the reassuring thump of the wheels. The plane skimmed on solidity, slowed itself, swung in a powerful turn and headed back the way it had come down. It crept now, toward the gray fronts of assembled buildings, with trucks and human figures

THE SCHOOL OF DARKNESS

there. "Keep your seats until the plane comes to a full halt," cautioned the voice.

But passengers were unclasping seat belts, pawing in luggage racks. John Thunstone sat where he was until the plane stopped and the voice announced as much. Still Thunstone waited until the first nervous press in the aisle had moved on. Then he rose into a gap among the debarkers. He towered, wide-shouldered, to take down his flight bag and his crook-handled, brown-blotched cane, then moved toward the exit. He wore checked trousers and a dark blue blazer. His face was square, with a trim black mustache. Black, too, was his carefully combed hair, with threads of silvery gray. There was a dent in his nose, to show where once it had been broken.

A pretty stewardess smiled to say that she hoped he had enjoyed his journey, that he would fly with that line again, and inevitably, "Have a good day." Thunstone followed the others into a sort of tunnel like the inside of a gigantic accordion. At the far end they came into a spacious chamber, brilliantly lighted, and out through a gate in a bright rail. More people waited there, loudly greeting passengers they recognized.

"Mr. Thunstone?"

That was a man of medium height and healthy-seeming medium build, holding out a welcoming hand, nowhere near as big as Thunstone's. Intelligent lines ran across his brow and down his cheeks. His eyes were three-cornered, like an athlete's.

"My name's Lee Pitt, I'm with the Department of English at Buford State," he introduced himself. "Since I teach a folklore course, I'm stuck, more or less, with this symposium on folklore and legend, and I thought I'd come meet you and drive you over."

"Thank you, Professor Pitt," said Thunstone, shaking

THE SCHOOL OF DARKNESS

hands. "It's kind of you. As soon as I pick my luggage up—"

"Downstairs," said Pitt.

An escalator took them to the level below. There, a U-shaped conveyor belt crawled like a mighty worm, bringing suitcases and parcels to view upon it. Men and women stepped close to pick these off. Thunstone waited until his big blue suitcase with its brown leather trim trundled into sight. He seized it and lifted it away as though it weighed nothing, and waited again to spy and claim its lesser mate. Pitt took the smaller case and led Thunstone out upon a paved gallery with a roof and supporting posts. Along the edge of this moved taxis, cars and pickup trucks, each stopping as someone heaved luggage aboard and then got in to roll away.

"Watch for a blue Chevy sedan with a dented left fender," said Pitt. "I won't be gone long."

He trotted across the driveway and into a great sea of parked cars. Thunstone watched his swift, sure movement and decided that Professor Lee Pitt would be an interesting acquaintance.

The blue sedan came and stopped at the curb. Pitt emerged from under the wheel to unlock the rear trunk, and Thunstone heaved his luggage in, but kept his cane as he got into the front seat with Pitt. They rolled away out of the airport and turned left on a paved secondary road.

"It's about twenty miles to Buford," said Pitt. "We'll make it by four o'clock. What do you want to know about Buford State University and the meeting?"

"As much as you can tell me," replied Thunstone, his great hands clamped on the crook of his cane. "I've heard of Buford, of course, the town and the school both, but this is my first visit here."

"Buford State University is about a hundred and fifty years old," said Pitt. "It started in an interesting way. Back

4 THE SCHOOL OF DARKNESS

then, before the Civil War, this was just a country village. A New England business man, Samuel Whitney, came in on some errand and took seriously ill. The doctor in town couldn't diagnose or treat his ailment, said he was going to die. But the people of Buford tried their best for that poor stranger. Some ladies prayed by his bedside every night. Maybe that was why he recovered. Anyway, he was deeply grateful and asked what he could do for the people who had saved his life. Someone or other—nobody today is sure who —said that Buford had always wanted a college."

"And Buford got one?" prompted Thunstone.

"Yes. It turned out that Samuel Whitney was very rich, very rich indeed. He gave them money, he paid for building a hall and then another one—those halls are still where he put them up. Whitney College struggled and survived, Whitney and some others he interested kept financing it. Well, many years passed. The town of Buford grew until it took over Whitney College, back in the 1930s, and named it Buford Municipal University. After that, it became part of the state's Consolidated University operation, and today it's Buford State."

Pitt's three-cornered eyes cut toward Thunstone as he drove. "Naturally," he said, "there's an old wives' tale connected with all this, and we don't lack old wives, or young ones either, to keep telling it."

"What's the tale?" asked Thunstone, immediately interested.

"They say that Whitney had been stricken down with some sort of curse," said Pitt. "To that they add, that those who prayed around his bed and brought him back to health weren't exactly church members—that they harked back to what we euphemistically call the Old Religion."

"Witchcraft," said Thunstone at once. "Diabolism."

"Something of the sort, and perhaps a school needs in-

THE SCHOOL OF DARKNESS

triguing old legends like that. Maybe there's some kernel of fact at the center of the thing."

"And maybe there's a coven operating on the grounds today," Thunstone offered.

Pitt shot him a quick glance, and turned the car upon a four-lane highway.

"Yes," he said. "I've heard about two covens. My folklore students assure me that they exist. One on campus, one off."

"Operating seriously?"

"Seriously enough, from what I hear. Of course, I've never been to any of their meetings. Maybe they do follow the ancient traditions. Or maybe they've just read a couple of paperbacks and think they know what the score is; more or less the way some students read the *Communist Manifesto* and think they're Marxist dialecticians."

"I'd like to hear more on the subject," said Thunstone. "What I do know of Buford State is a reputation for scholarship—the humanities, the sciences, law, music and so on. And you have a pretty good football team, too."

"We did all right in football last fall, and the fall before that," Pitt told him.

"What about your students in general?"

"We have eight thousand or so, including those in the graduate schools," said Pitt. "Quite a few of them as shaggy and untidy and noisy as small-time rock musicians. Then some serious, dedicated ones who want to be ministers or educators or junior business executives. And there are foreigners, of course—Germans, Filipinos, Asiatics and so on. And the athletic grant-in-aiders playing football and basketball. Speaking of which, haven't you played football in your time?"

"When I was in college, I did."

"I thought so, just by the way you walk. You certainly don't need that cane you carry."

6 THE SCHOOL OF DARKNESS

"I just carry it," said Thunstone. "It's a gift from an old friend."

"I was in athletics, too," said Pitt. "When I was at the University of Missouri, I wrestled. Now as to our meeting, it's attracted attention all through the country. Likewise, it's attracted some distinguished folklore authorities, like yourself."

"And like Reuben Manco, the Cherokee chief and medicine man," said Thunstone. "I've met him. He's highly civilized."

"He'll be at dinner with you tonight, Chancellor Pollock is entertaining all the star turns. There'll also be Professor Tashiro Shimada from Tokyo University, and Father Mark Bundren from New York. He's a scholarly Jesuit, deep in traditional lore—maybe as erudite as Montague Summers, though nothing like as credulous. At least, I don't think so. And, I believe, Grizel Fian of the Department of Dramatic Arts."

They rolled past filling stations, two motels, a restaurant promising excellent seafood.

"Grizel Fian," Thunstone repeated. "I don't think I know who she is."

"I doubt if many do know who she is," said Pitt. "She isn't officially of the faculty, not quite. But greatly interested in the D.A. Department, and she's written and directed plays there. I think she was once on the stage in New York."

"I don't remember hearing about her there," said Thunstone.

"Well, show business somewhere, anyway. Beyond that, she's somewhere in her forties, but a really spectacularly good-looking woman. I can't tell you if she's ever been married or not, but if you write her a letter or mention her in a newspaper story, it has to be Ms. Fian, and she wants to be called Ms. Fian."

THE SCHOOL OF DARKNESS 7

"How about the people who'll attend this meeting?" was Thunstone's next question.

"I can't say how many. Hundreds, anyway. Some visiting folklore professors, some scholars who'll hold seminars. And the students will want to come, and others."

"And others," said Thunstone.

They came to a shopping center where a sign said BUFORD CITY LIMITS. Past that, on either side of Main Street, stood big, impressive houses, lived in for nobody could say how many years. Then shops, then a bank and another bank, people treading the sidewalk. On the far side, a low wall and the green lawns of a campus; gigantic trees, a statue of somebody in some sort of uniform, and farther in, the lifted heads and shoulders of big Georgian brick buildings. Pitt braked to a stop at a crossing of principal streets, waited for the traffic light to change, and turned them to drive left past fraternity houses with big Greek letters on them, and finally into a parking lot behind a three-story sprawl of brick and stone. He nosed them into an empty space and shut off his motor.

"This is the Inn," he said. "Buford Inn. Let's go and get you squared off."

They got out and took Thunstone's luggage out of the trunk. They walked along a sort of colonnade to glass-fronted doors, then into a wide lobby. Guests sat and talked on sofas and armchairs. Pitt led the way to the desk at one end of the lobby and spoke to a plump, smiling girl.

"This is Mr. John Thunstone, who'll speak at our symposium," he said. "A reservation was made for him early in the week."

"Yes, Professor Pitt, we have the note here," she said, and struck a bell on the desk. A tall, coffee-brown man in a blue tunic with yellow trim came across the floor and picked up Thunstone's bags.

"We're glad to have you here, Mr. Thunstone," said the

8   THE SCHOOL OF DARKNESS

girl. "Oh, and you have mail." She handed him two envelopes. "We hope you'll be comfortable. If you want anything, call here at the desk."

"Thank you," he said.

"And now, I have to get back to work," Pitt said to Thunstone. "I feel like a prediction—people at this symposium will want to hear what you say more than what anyone else says."

"Then I'd better try to speak the truth," said Thunstone, smiling.

"Everybody should try to speak the truth."

Pitt went swiftly away. Thunstone followed the man with his luggage to an elevator. They rode up two floors and emerged into a red-carpeted corridor. The man put a key into the lock of a door that bore the number and let them in.

It was a room with off-white walls and doors and an off-white ceiling. Next to the window stood a broad bed, covered with a dark, patterned spread. Thunstone looked into a bathroom with a tub and a shower. The dark man set the larger suitcase on a rack and put the smaller one beside it.

"Will that be all, sir?" he asked.

"Could you find me some ice?"

"Right away, there's an ice machine down at the end of the hall."

The man went out. Thunstone took off his blazer and hung it in a closet. He loosened his necktie and opened his suitcase on the rack. The dark man came back in again, with a deep trayful of ice cubes. Thunstone thanked him, gave him a dollar, and shut the door behind him.

He looked at the watch on his wrist. It was a quarter after four.

From his larger suitcase he brought out a squat, square bottle of brandy. Plastic glasses stood on the bureau. He put a cube of ice in one, trickled brandy into it, took a sip. Then he looked at his two letters.

THE SCHOOL OF DARKNESS 9

One bore the return address of Judge Keith Hilary Pursuivant, and was postmarked at Richmond. He opened it and read:

My dear boy,

Even stricken in years as I am, I wish I could come there and hear what golden text you'll preach from at your meeting. What will your hearers think? Nobody believes anything these days, and everybody believes in something strange.

But I'm caught up here, trying to write my new book about the influence of supernatural beliefs on American culture. I tell practically everything except for my own life story, which is the sort of story that shouldn't be told.

When you're done with your duties there, why not come to visit? It's April, the mint's sprouting in my patch. I'll make you one of those juleps I learned the secret of in New Orleans, back when you were just a boy.

I say again, I wish I could be there. At that sort of a meeting, who can say what might break out and try to be direly effective?

On which disquieting note, I close by saying

Yours, etc.,
KHP

Thunstone mused, the letter in his hand. His old friend Pursuivant, still magnificent, still wise, still brilliantly scholarly in his eighties. Pursuivant, renderer of priceless but unappreciated service in both the world wars. Pursuivant, who had given him that walking stick that hid the silver blade. On impulse, Thunstone picked up the stick, turned the crooked handle, and freed the blade it held. Silver, that blade, gray ancient silver, said to have been forged for the

10 THE SCHOOL OF DARKNESS

master smith Saint Dunstan, a long thousand years ago. He traced the Latin letters still legible upon it:

Sic pereant omnes inimici tui, Domine. So perish all thine enemies, O Lord. How useful that blade had been, now and then in Thunstone's past.

He slid the blade back into its sheath, again sipped brandy, and took up the other letter. No return address this time, but instantly he knew the writing of his name and address upon it. This envelope, too, he opened.

Inside a card with just a single sentence in a clear, sure feminine hand:

Sooner than you think!
Sharon

Of course. She who had been Sharon Hill, who held the title of the Countess of Monteseco. From whom he had actually fled, again and again, trying to keep her from involvement in his perilous adventures. Thunstone frowned, but the frown was a tender one, a fond one.

The telephone rang, on the stand beside his chair. He picked it up. "Hello," he said.

"Thunstone?" a deep bass voice came to him.

"Yes," he said, "Thunstone here."

"It is better not."

A click as the connection was broken.

Thunstone put up his own instrument. Now his frown was neither tender nor fond.

What voice had spoken to him? He knew it from somewhere, but whose was it?

II

Thunstone pondered the question and could find no answer whatever. After a time, he stripped, went into the bathroom and showered, soaping his muscular body from head to foot. Then he shaved his square jaw, combed and parted his wet hair. He put on clean clothes, with a white shirt and a blue necktie sprinkled with white squares. His dark suit was conservative, but it had been skillfully cut by a good London tailor. Sitting down, he brought out a briar pipe, filled and lighted it, and thought.

The telephone rang again. He picked it up. "Hello."

"Mr. Thunstone?" said a man's voice, quite unrecognizable this time.

"Yes, sir."

"This is George Pollock. I'm the chancellor here at Buford State. I hope to see you at dinner tonight."

"Yes, thank you, Chancellor. Professor Pitt spoke about that."

"Shall we say six-thirty, then? We'll eat in the dining room at the Inn, and we can meet in the lobby. I'll recognize you, Mr. Thunstone, I've seen your picture in the New York papers. There'll be some other interesting people along."

"Will Professor Pitt be there?"

"No, Lee can't come. He'll be speaking tomorrow morning, and he's still deciding what to say. He's earnest about such things."

"Thank you," said Thunstone. "I'll be in the lobby."

12   THE SCHOOL OF DARKNESS

They both hung up. Thunstone got a flat envelope brief-case from his bag, and from that drew a printed program. AMERICAN FOLKLORE SURVEY SYMPOSIUM, said big black capital letters at the top. Below that, it showed the program for the first day, tomorrow, Friday, at Whitney Auditorium. At ten o'clock in the morning, the chancellor would make opening remarks. Then Lee Pitt would give an introductory speech and afterward would preside over a panel including John Thunstone, Chief Reuben Manco, Professor Tashiro Shimada and Father Mark Bundren, each of these dealing with studies of the supernatural. At 1 P.M., Manco would speak on myths and legends of the American Indian. Then, at 3:30 P.M., Father Bundren on Satanism. At 8 P.M., at the Playmakers Theater, would be presented scenes from William Shakespeare that dealt with the classic supernatural.

He saw that on Saturday, the final day, he and the others would appear on a morning panel with a question-and-answer period. At one o'clock, Pitt would speak on America's literature of the supernatural. At three o'clock, Professor Shimada would discuss Oriental beliefs and their influence on various national cultures. Finally, at eight o'clock in the evening, he, Thunstone, was to deliver the final address of the program.

The final address: he had better make it a good one. He looked at his watch. It was a quarter past six. He went out to the elevator and down to the lobby.

Knots of people stood and chatted here and there. One group looked up at Thunstone as he came into view. One of them, dark and wiry, raised his hand in recognition. Thunstone walked toward them.

A gaunt, gray-haired man stepped forward and held out his hand. "I'm George Pollock," he said. "Glad to see you, and so are these others. Grizel, may I present Mr. Thunstone. Ms. Grizel Fian, sir."

She stepped forward to face Thunstone. She was tall and

proud to look at; she wore a low-cut gown of soft blue material that clung to the splendid proportions of her figure. Her rich brown hair was drawn back into a bun. She had a handsome, ivory-pale face. Her red lips smiled as she looked at Thunstone with wide green eyes and gave him a slim, jeweled hand.

"How much I've looked forward to meeting you," she purred.

"And Chief Reuben Manco," said Pollock.

"We know each other," said the wiry man who had singled Thunstone out. His gray-black hair hung in two braids to bracket his brown, seamed face. "How are you, Thunstone?" he asked, and they shook hands.

"This is Father Mark Bundren," went on Pollock.

The priest wore clericals, dark suit and vest, with a round white collar. He was tall, though not as tall as Thunstone, and rather stocky without being soft. He had a short, straight nose, a good-humored mouth. His dark hair was closely curled.

"How do you do?" he said, giving Thunstone his hand. "I've heard about you, read about you. I hope to profit by talking to you."

"And this is Professor Tashiro Shimada."

Professor Shimada was a shred of a man, smaller than Manco. His face was leathery tan, with twinkling spectacles and a bristling gray mustache. His teeth gleamed whitely in a smile.

"Now, shall we go on into the dining room?" invited Pollock. "I've reserved a table for us and ordered a dinner I hope you will all like. Here, follow me."

He led them into the dining room. A white-jacketed waiter met them inside the door and conducted them to a table in a corner. Pollock pointed them to seats, with Grizel Fian at the head and himself and Thunstone at her right

14   THE SCHOOL OF DARKNESS

and left. Father Bundren sat at the opposite end of the table, and Shimada and Manco took chairs at either side of him.

The waiter brought steaming plates of onion soup, each with a slice of toasted French bread floating on top and a liberal sprinkling of grated Parmesan cheese. Thunstone tasted his. It was excellent, and both Father Bundren and Shimada praised it aloud. Grizel Fian ate hers with manifest appetite. Glancing up at Thunstone, she smiled warmly, almost conspiratorially. They finished the soup, and Pollock spoke.

"The subjects of folklore and legendry are universally interesting," he said, as though saying something new. "In all countries and among all cultures."

"I've thought that for a number of years," contributed Father Bundren. "More than that, they're also especially interesting to the classicist. Anyone who wants to laugh at them must be prepared to laugh at every religious faith in the world."

"Amen, if I may use a Christian locution when I worship the old Cherokee gods," put in Reuben Manco.

"Japanese culture is built upon a tremendous fabric of immemorial folk belief, and I hope to explain that here," said Shimada in his turn. His English had only a trace of accent.

"Father Bundren mentioned laughter, and we may hear some of that on this occasion," resumed Pollock. "There have already been several facetious newspaper stories here and there. Hundreds of people are coming, and not all of them with open minds. I depend on you gentlemen, yes and on you Grizel, to be highly impressive."

"We'll try," promised Manco, and, "We'll try," echoed Grizel Fian.

The waiter had carried the soup plates away. Now he returned with other plates that bore slices of roast beef, browned potatoes, broccoli. He filled glasses with bright red

THE SCHOOL OF DARKNESS

wine, and set a wooden bowl of shredded lettuce before Pollock.

"Will all of you start eating?" Pollock said to them. "I'm going to mix this salad, and if you don't like it, I'll cry."

He poured in olive oil from a cruet and stirred it judiciously with a wooden fork and spoon.

"I remember an ancient recipe for salad," offered Father Bundren. "You need a miser for the oil."

"I don't think I was exactly miserly," said Pollock, sprinkling salt and pepper and stirring those in, too. "But your recipe continues, a spendthrift for the vinegar."

He sluiced on a liberal portion of red wine vinegar.

"And a madman to stir it," pronounced Father Bundren.

"Exactly," said Pollock and stirred vigorously, then served out portions in smaller wooden bowls and handed them around. Grizel Fian tasted a forkful.

"You needn't cry on my account," she said. "It's beautiful."

Thunstone took some in his turn. "Amen," he said.

They ate the beef and the vegetables and the salad, all with good appetites. Meanwhile, they talked about the coming programs. Pollock asked if Father Bundren had ever exorcised evil spirits.

"I've done that from time to time," said Father Bundren. "Some of my work lies among people on the Lower East Side in New York. They call on me for exorcisms, and I perform them, and hope that they work."

"Don't you know if they work?" asked Grizel Fian quickly.

"It's hard to be sure of anything in an enigmatic world," was the priest's reply. "Yet there are certain phenomena— interesting, sometimes daunting. But I'll save those until I have to speak here."

"There has to be exorcism among the Cherokees," said Manco, buttering a fragment of roll. "We recognize evil and

16 THE SCHOOL OF DARKNESS

its spirits. We have the *anisgina*—malignant spirits of evil, and among them the worst are the Raven Mockers. If you happen to be sick or wounded, the Raven Mockers will come to suck your blood and kill you."

"Like vampires in the Old World," suggested Thunstone.

"You can find vampires in the New World, too," said Manco. "The New World is older, perhaps, than the Old. To drive the Raven Mockers away from a victim will take all a skilled medicine man has of prayer and method."

"You sound as if you've had it to do, Mr. Manco," remarked Grizel Fian.

"Frequently," Manco said, and no more than that. Carefully he cut a morsel of beef.

Pollock smiled. "Professor Shimada," he said, "these Occidental pronouncements must amuse a sophisticate of the Far East, from immemorial Japan."

Shimada smiled in his turn. "Sophistications are relative," he said gently, "and as for being immemorial, we Japanese aren't really that when we consider the long life of man on earth. Probably the first settlers of Japan came from what is now Korea, something like two hundred thousand years ago." He smiled again. "Earlier by some ages than the first adventurers to Australia or America, no more than fifty thousand years ago, if that."

"You make my people sound like parvenus," said Manco.

"No, no, your earliest Americans came from the Asiatic mainland, like the Japanese, like the Australians."

"And perhaps like my European ancestors," put in Thunstone. "I mean the first modern men in Europe, the Cro-Magnons. They may have come from Asia or even Africa, but they got there."

"I greatly admire the Cro-Magnon paintings," said Shimada. "But to speak of the supernatural, it's a prime factor in Japanese religious beliefs. I'm here to discuss that when I make my speech."

THE SCHOOL OF DARKNESS

"And you, Mr. Thunstone?" asked Grizel Fian.

She leaned toward him above the table. Her low-cut gown slid away from the upper slopes of her pale breasts. Her green eyes probed at him.

"Do you believe in what they call the supernatural?" she asked. "Is it possible?"

"If it's possible, it's not supernatural," he replied. "I believe in what I've experienced, in the work I've done all my life. People talk to me about impossibilities and possibilities, but I feel that the old saying fits in somehow, that a likely impossibility is always preferable to an unconvincing possibility."

"Whoever said such a thing?" inquired Pollock.

"Aristotle did, for one," said Manco, before Thunstone could speak.

The waiter took away their plates and brought back slices of Black Forest torte and a pot of coffee. As they ate their dessert, they continued to talk of various beliefs and their influence. At last they were finished. Pollock and Grizel Fian and Shimada lighted cigarettes. Thunstone and Father Bundren produced briar pipes, and Manco brought out an Indian pipe of dark red stone, carved to resemble an elephant.

"How interesting, your pipe," said Grizel Fian to him. "An elephant shape to it."

"It was made by my ancestors, long before Columbus came to America," he told her.

"But an elephant?" she protested. "There weren't any elephants in America then."

"Thousands of years before Columbus, there were elephants in America," Manco said.

"True," seconded Father Bundren.

Again Grizel Fian leaned herself toward Thunstone, giving him another glimpse of her bosom.

18   THE SCHOOL OF DARKNESS

"Mr. Thunstone," she said, "do you remember a man named Rowley Thorne?"

"I remember him very clearly," he answered her.

"You do? And where is he now?"

"As to that, I can't really say. The last time we were together, I saw him vanish."

"Vanish?" repeated Pollock, interested. "Into thin air, you mean?"

"I don't know where he vanished to, but he was gone," said Thunstone evenly. "He'd failed at something he tried to do, and the things he had summoned didn't have any use for failures. They went back to whatever place they'd come from, and apparently they took Rowley Thorne along, and I've heard nothing of him since."

"You're having fun with us!" Pollock almost cried at him.

"No," said Thunstone. "I'm telling what seemed at the time to be the truth."

"Vanish?" said Pollock again. "You don't know where. What sort of man was this Rowley Thorne?"

"Physically he was a big man, as big as I am," Thunstone said. "Bald-headed, or perhaps closely shaved all over his skull. Strong, prominent features. That's what he looked like. As for the rest—perhaps you'd like to describe that, Ms. Fian."

"Very wise," she said, almost prayerfully. "Very deeply versed in strange sciences."

"But where did he go?" persisted Pollock. "Into some other dimension, are you trying to say?"

"Science recognizes other dimensions," said Thunstone patiently. "Mysticism recognizes other planes. I don't pretend to be fully informed about these things, but"—he fixed Grizel Fian with his eyes—"I'm relieved and glad that he's gone."

"Maybe he's not gone," she said, so softly that he could barely hear.

THE SCHOOL OF DARKNESS

"Well, all this is strange, it's very interesting," vowed Pollock. "Now, does anyone here wish anything else I can get for you?"

"For myself, I'd be glad to be excused," said Manco, rising. "I'm to be on the panel with you others tomorrow morning, and later I must speak all alone, and I want to go over the things I must speak about."

They all got up, smiling at each other. They thanked Pollock for his hospitality and promised to see him the next morning. Then they started away into the lobby and through it. Grizel Fian walked along with Thunstone. Her shoulder touched his briefly.

"You're so sure that Rowley Thorne vanished," she whispered conspiratorially.

"I saw him vanish," said Thunstone. "He vanished like an image from a screen when the light goes off."

"Where did he go?" she asked. Her eyes were like green lamps. "Where?"

"One lesson I've learned from the life I've led, is not to inquire too importunately into things like that. What are you trying to say? Do you think that he's returned from wherever it was?"

"I'll want to talk to you again."

She turned away and crossed the lobby toward a door on the far side. She winnowed as she walked. Watching, Thunstone thought he saw her make a motion to a man beside the door.

That man was powerfully built, big-nosed. He wore a checked sports coat. His head was as bald as a great egg.

Then Shimada was at Thunstone's elbow. "Chief Manco and I, we have rooms on the fourth floor," he said. "Would you like to come with us? I look forward to more discussion with you."

"Perhaps in a little while, Professor," said Thunstone. "I

20 THE SCHOOL OF DARKNESS

have some things to note down in my own room. What's your number?"

Shimada looked at the tag of his key. "Room 412," he said.

They went up together in the elevator. Thunstone got off at the third floor, strode quietly along the corridor to his room. As he unlocked the door, he heard the telephone ringing. He entered swiftly and picked up the instrument. "Hello," he said.

"Hello yourself," said a gentle voice he knew at once. "You're hard to find at home. I've called and called."

"Sharon!" he almost shouted. "Where are you calling from?"

"Why," said Sharon, Countess Monteseco, quite easily, "right here in this Inn. I'm about two doors away from you. Room 316."

"Come here to 312 at once."

"You make that sound rather like an assignation," she said, "but I'll come at once."

She hung up. John Thunstone hung up, too, and sat and thought about her. They had not seen each other in years, but she was vivid in his memory.

Countess Monteseco, who once had been the golden girl called Sharon Hill. Who had been drawn to Thunstone but had been a trifle afraid of his strange adventuring, who had gone abroad and had married Count Monteseco of Italy. Count Monteseco's title had been only an empty one in that nation which had become a democracy after Mussolini, and Count Monteseco had been a troublesome, sinister man who, when he had died, had not seemed to die too soon. Monteseco was still her name but once she had been Sharon Hill.

A knock at the door. "It's open," he called, and in she came.

Sharon, Countess Monteseco, was pleasantly handsome. Her hair was blond, with a touch of red, what some called

THE SCHOOL OF DARKNESS

strawberry blond. She wore a tailored suit of brown-and-green-checked twill, with a scarf at her throat. Her figure was compactly symmetrical; she had a fine arched nose and wide curved lips and eyes a trifle bluer than sapphires. If she was beautiful, it was not the beauty of a doll or of a siren. She smiled as she entered, with the closed-lipped smile associated with the Mona Lisa and the Empress Josephine.

She held out her small, strong hand to Thunstone. He took it and kissed it.

"For God's sake, what are you doing here?" he asked at once.

"Why, the New York papers said that you'd be the principal speaker at this meeting." She smiled back at him. "I came to hear you, to be with you. Why? Aren't you glad to see me?"

Her smile waited, but he frowned.

"Sharon," he said, "there's never been a time when I wasn't glad to see you. But if you're here, you're in danger. Remember Rowley Thorne?"

"Yes," she said, "yes, but isn't he gone?"

"I have a notion that he's here." He motioned to a chair, and she sat down. He sat on the bed and leaned toward her. "Time after time I've had to save you from things the world doesn't believe can exist. I've always wanted you to keep clear, stay out of danger."

Now she frowned, a tiny crease between her brows. "Well," she said after a moment. "I hadn't expected this sort of a reception. Am I wrong in remembering that you used to say you loved me?"

"I do love you, this minute I love you," he fairly burst out. "I've always loved you, since first we met, since before you went abroad and married your Italian count."

"That's all I want to know," she half whispered.

She, too, leaned forward, put her small hands on his big shoulders and met his mouth with a strong, swimming kiss.

22 THE SCHOOL OF DARKNESS

Thunstone took her close in his arms and returned the kiss with a burning hunger. But then he released her and stood up, away from where she sat.

"There," the countess said. "Maybe I was a trifle shameless, but didn't I convince you that I can love, too?"

"Yes," he said, rather gruffly. "But I say again, you're in peril here. That always happens when you're with me. I mentioned Rowley Thorne."

"Isn't he gone?" she reminded him again. "Vanished into nowhere? You told me that."

"He vanished, and I'd hoped forever. He brought a whole army of evil spirits against me, and when I defeated them they disappeared, and took Thorne with them."

"How can that happen?"

"It seems to happen all the time. Ambrose Bierce made a study of disappearances, and he disappeared himself, without leaving a trace. Men and women seem to pop out of sight, before the eyes of witnesses. About a hundred years ago, a man named David Lang disappeared in a Tennessee field while his wife and two friends watched. These things happen."

"Yes, and those planes dropping out of sight in the Bermuda Triangle, and the crew of the *Marie Celeste*," added the countess, her voice troubled. "But Rowley Thorne?"

"I'm fairly sure I saw him downstairs in the lobby," said Thunstone, "and I think he called me on the telephone earlier today."

"But nobody comes back from those disappearances," she argued.

"A man in the Carolina mountains, a man named Sol Gentry, seemed to fade out of existence in sight of his home," said Thunstone. "Twenty years or so later, he was there again, at the very same spot. He didn't remember anything about being gone, but he was back."

Her face had gone pale. "Then—"

"Thorne seems to be here, Sharon. And he knows I'm here, and probably knows that you're here, too. He's always wanted you for a victim, hasn't he?"

"Why does he want me? Why?"

Thunstone reached a long arm to the side table. He took the brandy bottle and poured drinks into two glasses and handed her one.

"Let me speak to the point, Sharon," he said. "You haven't been wise about him all the time, but he's paid considerable intelligent attention to you. I'd diagnose the situation like this: Thorne is evil. He's spent his life being evil, he's brought a considerable talent to it. As for you, you're a fundamentally good, normal woman. He recognizes that. And evil wants to conquer good, overthrow it."

Her glass trembled in her hand as she sipped. She said, "What you say sounds fantastic, but I believe you. I always believe what you say."

"Because you know that I always mean what I say." He finished his drink and rose. "Now, you're in Room 316, two doors away from me, but I can't be here all the time. Let me give you this protection."

He searched in his suitcase and brought out a piece of reddish brown twig, set on both sides with half-dried elliptical leaflets. He gave it to her.

"That's rowan," he told her. "Mountain ash. I want you to hang it inside your door. It's a protection against lots of evil things."

"But I have a charm already, John." She, too, got up, put a hand inside her scarf, and brought out a small golden cross on a golden chain. "Do you recognize this? You gave it to me, and I always wear it. I never take it off except to take a bath."

"Use the rowan, too," he urged her. "Don't overlook any bets, Sharon. And now I'll walk you to your door, look into your room to see that everything's all right, and come back here to do some thinking."

24   THE SCHOOL OF DARKNESS

"Why can't I stay here with you for a while?"

Thunstone smiled, and the smile brought out deep lines around his mouth.

"Because if you stay, it'll be hard for me to think profitably."

Her own mouth pouted, for just a moment. "Well," she said, "all right."

They walked out together. The countess put her key in the lock of Room 316. Thunstone entered with her. He looked at the window, uncapped his pen, and drew a cross on the off-white sill. He hung the branch of rowan above the door.

"I sat down in your room," she said. "Won't you sit down in mine?"

"I can't, I told you I have thinking to do."

They came close, their arms went around each other. They kissed. Never, said Thunstone to himself, had they kissed like that.

"You didn't seem to be away from me just then," she chided him.

"I'd dearly love to be with you, somewhere else than here," he said, still holding her against him. "Somewhere else, where perils didn't loom up." He released her. "Now, go to bed early. In the morning, as soon as you wake up, call me in Room 312. We can go down to breakfast together."

"I hope it will be a good breakfast," she smiled, "and that you're in a more cheerful mood."

"I'll try to be. Lock me out as I go, and keep your door locked."

Out in the hall, he gazed both ways along the corridor. He thought he saw shadows. Just shadows. He entered his room and locked himself in.

From his briefcase he took a pad of lined yellow paper. He uncapped his pen and began to make notes.

III

Thunstone was slow, was careful with the notes he set down. He frowned over them. Opposite one note, then opposite two others, he wrote question marks. He spent hours at what he wrote, and at last read the jottings over to himself. They might be a help.

He stopped, got into bed and yawned. It had been a tiring day, on the plane, at the various discussions, at the hints of strange peril. Swiftly he went to sleep, and did not stir until the telephone rang beside him.

He reached for it. "Hello," he said.

"Did I wake you up?" asked Sharon Monteseco's voice.

"You did, but I'm wide awake now. Let's meet in the hall and go to breakfast."

"As soon as I get on my clothes."

"As soon as I get on mine," he said. When he hung up, he found himself smiling and knew that the smile was a happy one. The sense of danger was there, for himself and for Sharon. Yet he would rather be with Sharon than anyone else on earth.

They met in the corridor and sought the automatic elevator. As they went down, Sharon suddenly straightened and stared. "Who's in here with us?" she stammered.

"Nobody," said Thunstone. "Just a shadow there in the corner."

To himself he wondered what invisible thing might have cast that shadow.

26 THE SCHOOL OF DARKNESS

They walked together through the lobby below and into the dining room and sat down at a table for two.

A waiter came. Sharon asked for a soft-boiled egg, a toasted muffin, and a cup of tea. Thunstone ordered scrambled eggs, country sausage, toast and coffee. Sharon smiled at him. "You always eat well," she said, "but you never get fat, all those big bones and muscles, but no extra flesh."

"Maybe I worry it off," he said.

Their food came and they ate. Then they rose and Thunstone put down money for the bill and a tip. "And now what?" asked Sharon.

"Today's program starts at ten o'clock, in the Whitney Auditorium, wherever that may be. Chancellor Pollock will open things with a brief address of welcome. After that, a panel discussion of the supernatural. It's chaired by Professor Lee Pitt, a man I think you'll like, and I'll be a member of the panel."

"I'll come and hear that," vowed Sharon.

"We'll go there together, and I'll see you to a seat close to the front, where I can keep an eye on you. All right, after the panel's heard from, a discussion period, questions and answers. Then at one-thirty in the afternoon Reuben Manco discusses supernormal matters among American Indians."

"Reuben Manco?" she repeated.

"A Cherokee chieftain and medicine man, graduate of Dartmouth, extremely wise. He's a friend of mine. Then, at half-past three, Father Mark Bundren on the prevalence of witchcraft and diabolism here and there today. You'll like him too, I think. And at night, at eight o'clock, a theatrical presentation at the Playmakers Theater. Shakespeare, I believe, various creepy sequences from his plays."

"Everything sounds diverting."

In the lobby, Thunstone spoke to the bell captain, who told him that Whitney Auditorium was on campus, just across the street in front of the Inn. They walked out and

THE SCHOOL OF DARKNESS

across, found a big square building of tawny brick, with massive pillars in front. As they entered the auditorium, Thunstone heard someone call him by name. In the aisle were grouped Lee Pitt, Shimada, Manco and Father Bundren.

Thunstone led Sharon to join them and introduced them to her, one after another. Shimada wore natty tweeds and smiled and bowed. Father Bundren, in his clericals, greeted Sharon as ceremoniously as a Renaissance cardinal. Pitt, too, was cordial. Manco, very dignified and deep-voiced, was the most elaborately dressed of the party. He wore a long hunting shirt of pale buckskin, fringed at sleeves and collar, with beadwork designs. His head was bound at the temples with a leather band, also beautifully beaded.

"We have about ten minutes, and people are coming in fast," said Pitt. "Where would you like to sit, Countess?"

"Somewhere close to the front," she replied. "Mr. Thunstone wants to keep an eye on me."

"Nor do I blame him for that," said Pitt. "How about here, right on the aisle. Is that all right?"

She smiled and took her seat, and Pitt led Thunstone and the others through a side door and up four steps to the wings. From there they could see the stage. Several tables were set there end to end, with chairs behind them and upon them microphones and a pitcher of water and glasses.

Chancellor Pollock came from behind a backstage curtain to join them. "The hall's filling up fast, gentlemen," he said. "Let's go out there and maybe we can start a program on time for once."

They followed him onstage, and a brisk clapping of hands greeted them. Pitt took the chair at the middle of the line of tables and motioned Shimada and Thunstone to his right, Father Bundren and Manco to his left. Pollock waited for the applause to die down, then moved to stand beside Pitt and take up the microphone that stood on the table there.

28 THE SCHOOL OF DARKNESS

He spoke, and his amplified voice filled the auditorium. "Ladies and gentlemen and distinguished visitors," he said, "I won't make anything that you could call a speech. I'll say only, welcome to the American Folklore Survey Symposium. Your printed programs will tell you about our sessions today and tomorrow. And now, permit me to turn this present meeting over to Professor Lee Pitt, and I'll come sit among you and listen."

Thunstone looked at Sharon. She sat no more than thirty feet from him. Her eyes were on him. She smiled her close-lipped smile.

Pitt took back the microphone and spoke in turn. "We have here a distinguished group of authorities on the subjects of folklore and legendry," he said. "Like Chancellor Pollock, I won't make a long lecture here—I'm directed to lecture at a later session. Let me introduce each of my companions in turn, and each will say what he feels like saying. When all are through, we'll welcome any questions from the audience."

He turned and looked to his right. "First, I'll recognize a deservedly eminent educator from Tokyo University, Professor Tashiro Shimada. I have long profited by his writings, and whatever he has to say this morning will surely be worth hearing." He nodded. "Professor Shimada."

Again applause. Shimada acknowledged it with a toothy smile and a brief bob of his head. His spectacles twinkled. Then he began, in his precise English with only the trace of an accent:

"Ladies and gentlemen, Professor Pitt embarrasses me with his flattery. It is true that I am a professor myself, have studied Oriental folklore for many years, and have contributed to the literature of the subject. I hope that I come to you, not simply as a Japanese, but as a cosmopolitan. I have studied in many Asiatic lands—in China, India, even the

THE SCHOOL OF DARKNESS

Arab countries. Everywhere, I found strong beliefs in amazing things, and strong evidence to support those beliefs."

As he went on with remarks on ancient and modern Eastern religions and legends, Thunstone quartered the thronged auditorium with his eyes. He looked at Sharon, who again smiled at him. He found Grizel Fian, seated midway in the center section. She wore a dark red dress that made her stand out in the crowd. In the seat behind her was the figure of a burly man. Thunstone could see his bald head, like the head of . . .

"Later, I hope to go into more detail about beliefs in my native Japan," Shimada finished, and made his slight bow.

Pitt spoke again: "Next to Professor Shimada sits Mr. John Thunstone. From what I've been able to learn about him, he's a man who does not like to bring attention upon himself. Now and then, his activities have found their way into the newspapers. He is greatly respected by several societies for psychical research, though I don't find that he belongs to any of them. May I present Mr. Thunstone?"

Thunstone drew the microphone close to him and stooped his massive head close. "Thank you, Professor Pitt. I follow Professor Shimada's scholarly remarks with some diffidence. Yet I'm reminded of what was once written by a man of a very ordinary name, John Smith. It was Captain Smith who kept Jamestown in Virginia from being a lost colony like the one on Roanoke Island in Carolina. A letter came from London, complaining that his reports did not agree with those of scholars at home, and he wrote back that though he was no scholar, he was yet past a schoolboy, risking his life to learn what he could of a land of perilous mystery."

Shimada chuckled softly beside him.

"I take further refuge with another favorite historical figure of mine, Lord Byron," Thunstone went on. "Once he said, 'Truth is always strange—stranger than fiction,' and

THE SCHOOL OF DARKNESS

others have been echoing him ever since. That's an important truth about truth. Just now I'll touch only briefly on things I've felt to be the truth, and you're welcome to believe them or not." He smiled. "As though I said I'd seen an unknown flying object or a fire-breathing dragon, or the ghost of Napoleon Bonaparte. First of all, does anyone here know what a Shonokin is?"

As he spoke, he shook his head warningly at Sharon, and she did not hold up her hand. But one hand did go up, a broad, heavy hand. It belonged to the burly man sitting behind Grizel Fian.

"I'll tell you what a Shonokin is," Thunstone continued. "Shonokins claim to be a race that was here in America before the first Asiatics crossed the Bering Strait and became Indians. They look prosaically human enough, except that the pupils of their eyes are slits instead of circles, and their third fingers are longer than their middle fingers. Are any Shonokins present?" He waited, looking at the audience again. One or two giggles were audible, rather nervous giggles. "I sit here and say that I've been face to face with Shonokins, have seen several of them die. And when a Shonokin dies, all living Shonokins flee away in terror."

Again he paused. Then: "Perhaps I'll have more to say about Shonokins at a later session of this symposium. As for other improbabilities, I can vouch for werewolves and vampires. I've come up against both of those creatures. But possibly you'll want to ask me questions about that."

He finished, and Pitt was back at his own microphone. "Next in line, let me introduce Chief Reuben Manco. Chief Manco is a Cherokee, and he is also a medicine man of his tribe. A sophisticate, too; he graduated from Dartmouth with honors, and he writes interestingly for various journals of history and folklore. Here he is."

"Thank you," said Manco deeply into his own microphone. Looking at him from the side, Thunstone saw the

THE SCHOOL OF DARKNESS

sweep of his curved nose, his square jaw, the brown strength of his face. "Last night," he said, "Professor Shimada observed that his ancestors were in Japan many thousands of years before mine were in America. I recognize that seniority, but I take leave to remark that my ancient people had a far larger area to explore and live in. And I also take leave to wonder if his Japanese civilization was established earlier than native civilizations in North and South America."

Shimada smiled and made a silent gesture of applause. Manco let his words sink in, then went on:

"There are old Indian beliefs in dazzling wonders—the Dreadful Rabbit, the menacing little Pukwitchee people, the Thunderbird that will send down rain if you know the right song to sing, the Half Buffalo creature that sounds like the Cretan Minotaur—people smile at these legends. Yet to every utterly strange belief there is, somewhere back at the beginning, a core of plain truth. There have been dragons in America—science calls them dinosaurs—even flying dragons, with wing spreads of fifty feet—their bones have been found in Texas. And sun gods and moon gods and spider fairies and grasshopper imps. Indians who believed in such things built civilizations in Mexico, in Yucatán and Peru." Manco permitted himself a hard, dry grin. "Who can certainly say, here or elsewhere—if Columbus had waited a few more centuries before he discovered America, what great triumphs of culture might have been realized by the Aztecs and the Mayas and the Peruvian Incas? A good question, don't you agree, and what might be the answer?"

The whole great audience listened raptly. He went on:

"I'm a Cherokee, as you've heard Professor Pitt say. I belong to one of what they call the Civilized Tribes. When I speak at greater length here, I'll go into the beliefs of my people, and I'll try to demonstrate how true some of those beliefs can be."

32 THE SCHOOL OF DARKNESS

He finished, and lifted a hand, palm out as though in blessing. Pitt returned to his own microphone.

"And last," he said, "let me introduce Father Mark Bundren, of New York City. Father Bundren is a classicist of high reputation, he is of the powerful, learned Society of Jesus founded by Saint Ignatius Loyola. He has been a teacher in Catholic colleges and universities, and now he is more widely active as a scholar of the occult. His books and articles on classic demonology are read and respected everywhere. Father Bundren, the floor is yours."

Some of the listeners stirred in their seats. Father Bundren smiled and began:

"Professor Pitt is pleased to say some flattering things. Let me say that I am simply a priest of my church, one of more than fifty thousand Catholic priests in the United States alone. And I venture to hope that, yes, I'm a classicist of sorts. I'll go along with what Mr. Thunstone has said for himself, I've experienced strange things in my life, and I feel obliged to believe in those strange things, to cope with them as I'm able. Diabolism is as ancient as man himself. Perhaps devils were worshiped and feared before gods—perhaps gods are relatively new among us on earth as compared to devils. As far back as the Stone Age, sorcerers flourished; we have their horned portraits in old, old caves. The pagans of Greece and Rome respected and served sorcerers. When Christianity dawned, it had diabolists to meet and defeat. Saint Peter, once named Simon, had a lively struggle with his namesake, Simon Magus. If we credit the writings of certain saints, Simon Magus tried to impress the Emperor Nero by soaring into the air. Saint Peter prayed, and Simon Magus fell crashing to the ground—he was killed, says one account. But his teachings didn't die with him. As late as the middle of the nineteenth century, there were Simon Magus cults both in America and in France."

THE SCHOOL OF DARKNESS

He was silent for a moment, while all the auditorium was silent. Then he went on:

"Witchcraft was sternly attacked in the Middle Ages and on into recent times. I gather that thousands of devil worshipers were executed. Maybe innocent people were among them, but there were witch doctors aplenty on the lists. We know about the Salem executions here. Other events of the sort happened elsewhere in our country. Today the law provides that no sincere religious belief can be forbidden or molested, and there are many, many professed witch organizations from coast to coast. I hope to go more deeply into this sort of thing later in our program here."

He, too, finished, and Pitt said, "We will now hear any questions anyone cares to ask, and will try to answer them. Hold up your hands. When you're recognized, state your name and offer your query."

Then silence. To Thunstone, it seemed a heavy silence. After a moment, hands went up here and there. Pitt pointed to someone in the center section, and a young man stood up. He had long black hair and a small mustache. To Thunstone, he seemed to have a far-off resemblance to a tallish Edgar Allan Poe.

"My name's Exum Layton," said the man, his voice faint in the auditorium. "I'm a graduate student in English. I want to ask Mr. Thunstone, why do you say you believe in these phenomena?"

"Seeing is believing," said Thunstone into his microphone. "When you see something, experience something at first hand, it becomes reality to you and perhaps you can deal with it."

"You mentioned the Shonokins," Exum Layton said. "I've heard of them, but I thought they were fiction."

"They're real enough, in their seemingly unreal way," said Thunstone.

"I'd like to talk to you about them."

34 THE SCHOOL OF DARKNESS

"Very well, you may. I'm staying at the Inn, you can telephone me there."

Exum Layton sat down. Pitt pointed toward another lifted hand, a slim, white one. Grizel Fian rose from her seat.

"Yes," prompted Pitt.

"Mr. Thunstone," she said, and her voice was clearer, more resounding, than Layton's had been. "Last night, you and I spoke of Rowley Thorne. Would you like to tell us about him?"

Behind her sat the big man with the bald head. Thunstone could make out his face, heavy-jowled, hook-nosed.

"Rowley Thorne was, in his time, the world's principal figure in the cult of Satanism," said Thunstone at once. "He had various disciples, who gave him money to spend and supported his claims and actions. He didn't like me, and I didn't like him. One day, he vanished. I conjecture that he failed at some rather sinister magical effort, and got taken into some other plane of existence, away from the one we know."

A murmur rose among the listeners. "Do you believe that such a thing happened?" Grizel Fian half challenged.

"I saw it happen," Thunstone replied. "There are reports of such things in the past. I daresay that Father Bundren could give you some instances out of the Bible. I wouldn't be surprised if Professor Shimada could tell about such disappearances in Asia, or if Chief Manco could speak to them among Indian peoples."

"Thank you," said Grizel Fian, and sat down. The bald head behind her leaned close as though to speak in her ear. Pitt pointed to another in the audience, a middle-aged man this time, who rose and called himself Hollis Buchanan.

"I'm a member of no church, and I follow no religion," he said gratingly. "I ask Father Bundren how science can explain the curious things he believes in."

THE SCHOOL OF DARKNESS   35

"By and large, science doesn't recognize those things and doesn't try to explain them," was Father Bundren's cheerful answer. "Proof and faith are opposite paths of belief."

"Nothing is true without scientific proof," insisted Hollis Buchanan.

"Well, from time to time science catches up with things, with bewildering realities." Father Bundren smiled in a way that made his canny face look chubby. "I have said that I'm a priest, and I'll add that I'm not unacquainted with scientific theories that have become recognized facts. But, if I'm to do my duty as a priest, I can't help but believe in miracles and wonders. Those happen to be part of a priest's business."

Hollis Buchanan did not look particularly satisfied, but he sat down. Others raised their hands and asked questions, of Thunstone and all the others, and were answered as simply and clearly as possible. Most of the questioners wanted to know if members of the panel truly believed in supernormal phenomena, and if so, why. It occurred to Thunstone that he and his fellow panelists had no more than hinted at the matters they would discuss more fully later. At last, at about half past eleven, Pitt declared the session at an end.

"At one-thirty this afternoon, Chief Manco will be here to tell about the legendry of his great Cherokee nation," he announced. "Later, at three-thirty, Father Bundren will take up the subject of historical demonology. Thank you all for your attention."

He rose, and the members of the panel rose with him. The audience stirred and sought the aisles. Grizel Fian glittered as she moved. Thunstone caught Sharon's eye, gestured to her, and quickly left the stage and joined her.

"I've seen Rowley Thorne," were the first words she said to him, softly and unsteadily.

"And so have I, I believe," he said. "Well, if he's really

36 THE SCHOOL OF DARKNESS

here, he must be dealt with. I'll have to decide. Would you like some lunch at the Inn?"

"Yes. Yes, I would. I feel frightened just now, but I feel hungry, too."

They went out to the street corner, waited for a traffic light, and crossed over. Together they sought the dining room and sat down and looked at the menus brought by a waiter. They ordered shrimp salad and black coffee.

A voice spoke to them. Grizel Fian had come to stand beside their table. Her red silk dress shone.

"May I sit down with you two?" she asked. "I have something to say that might interest you."

IV

Thunstone was on his feet at once. "Of course," he said. "Please sit down with us. We're having lunch, will you have something?"

"Thank you, but no." Grizel Fian shook her head vigorously. "I don't eat lunch, I never do. Well—perhaps a cup of tea?"

"I'll get you one," said Thunstone. He pulled out a chair for her, and she sat down. Then he beckoned to the waiter and he ordered the tea. "Sharon, may I present Ms. Grizel Fian? And this is the Countess Monteseco, Ms. Fian."

Sharon nodded and smiled. Grizel Fian looked at her keenly. She almost stared.

"This is a pleasure," she said. "I've heard of you, Countess. I've heard that you were beautiful, and you are."

"Thank you," said Sharon.

"And I listened to you this morning," Grizel Fian almost burst out at Thunstone. "You said you'd encountered werewolves and vampires, and that strange race of the Shonokins. You sound as though you'll accept wonderful truths, believe in things that many people just scoff at. I came here—intruded here, really—to tell you something about the founding of this university."

"I'll be glad to hear about it," Thunstone assured her.

The waiter brought their lunch and set a cup and a small teapot before Grizel Fian. She poured her tea. Sharon and Thunstone began to eat.

"What I have to tell is laughed at sometimes, but the

38 THE SCHOOL OF DARKNESS

story hangs on here," said Grizel Fian. "It's about Samuel Whitney, who founded the school, and how he was taken strangely ill when he got here to Buford."

"Professor Pitt mentioned that interesting tale to me," said Thunstone.

"A tale, you call it." She leaned toward him, bright-eyed. "Calling it a tale makes it sound like some sort of a myth, a legend. But there's evidence—"

She broke off, and her full lips trembled.

"What sort of evidence?" prompted Sharon.

"The town used to say, Samuel Whitney had made certain people up North angry," said Grizel Fian. "He found himself to be suffering, to be sick, and he came here from wherever he'd been living, to get away from it. But whatever the plague was, it followed him and struck him down, and some kind people of Buford cared for him."

"Kind people?" Thunstone repeated after her. "What kind of kind people were they?"

"They were a group of Buford women who followed the Old Religion," said Grizel Fian.

"A coven of witches," supplied Thunstone, and Sharon's wide blue eyes grew wider.

"All right," nodded Grizel Fian. "A coven, if you want to call it that. You know what a coven is, Mr. Thunstone. There have been covens, like the one at North Berwick in Scotland."

"Yes, that famous one at North Berwick," he said. "By way of coincidence, the chief of that coven was named Fian, the same name as yours." He looked at her face, paler now than ever. "Could he have been a relative?"

"Who could know that, after four hundred years?" she said. "But those women here, they were kindly women, wise women. They prayed. They performed rituals. They saved Samuel Whitney's life. And in gratitude he founded the college here."

THE SCHOOL OF DARKNESS

"Yes," Sharon half whispered.

"Tell me, what agreement was made?" Thunstone asked. "They saved Whitney from whatever danger threatened him—did he promise them the college then, or did he found it later, in gratitude?" He smiled, ever so thinly. "In other words, was the college founded in the name of witchcraft?"

"Who knows that for certain, either?" asked Grizel Fian in turn. "I've told you this story to show that the Old Religion can help. It can heal. It can do good deeds."

"I've been told that there are at least two active covens here in Buford," said Thunstone. He chose not to add that Lee Pitt was his informant.

"Two?" said Grizel Fian after him. "At least two? Did you come here to see that they'd be investigated—prosecuted?"

"As I understand the interpretation of United States law by high federal and state courts, no coven can be challenged for what it believes," said Thunstone. "That happens to be guaranteed by the First Amendment to the Constitution— free exercise of religious belief, right along with freedom of speech or of the press, or of peaceable assembly. I'd say that a coven could meet and worship at high noon on the Main Street of Buford or any other town, if it didn't break any of various other laws, say a law against public nudity."

"Yes," said Grizel Fian, finishing her cup of tea. "Yes, of course. Now, another question. How well did you know Rowley Thorne, Mr. Thunstone?"

"I knew him very well indeed. As I said at the meeting this morning, we didn't like each other."

"Do you know if he's alive or dead?" Grizel Fian prodded.

"I'm not sure. As I said, I saw him disappear."

"Disappear," Sharon repeated in what sounded like awe.

"Before my very eyes," Thunstone went on. "What happened to him is beyond my comprehension."

40 THE SCHOOL OF DARKNESS

"So there's something beyond your comprehension, after all," said Grizel Fian, and she seemed to mock.

"There are many things beyond my comprehension," said Thunstone, smiling.

Grizel Fian leaned at him. "If you should see him come back to meet you, might you possibly make peace?"

Again Thunstone smiled. "That would depend on the peace terms," he replied. "I wouldn't expect unconditional surrender on either side. Why do you ask that?"

"You must forgive me for wondering about things," said Grizel Fian. "I do so much wondering."

"You're with the Department of Dramatic Arts here, aren't you?" asked Sharon.

Grizel Fian shook her head. "Not exactly. I'm not a bona fide instructor, I draw no salary, if that's what you mean. But they let me be actively interested. I direct plays sometimes—once or twice I've written plays, and staged them, too."

"I hear that you're actively interested in students, too," put in Thunstone. "That you let some girls stay in your home, and charge them no rent."

Grizel Fian opened her green eyes at him. "Mr. Thunstone, you seem to have asked questions about me."

"Let's say I've only listened to what people tell me," he said, still smiling.

"Very well," she said quickly. "I've tried to be a friend to girl students who need help here, who deserve it. Isn't that all right?"

"I haven't suggested that it wasn't," said Thunstone evenly.

"But now I must go. I have a show to present tonight. I hope you'll both come."

"We'll be there," Sharon promised.

Grizel Fian stood up. She fixed her eyes on Sharon.

THE SCHOOL OF DARKNESS 41

"I wish you could be in a scene tonight," she said. "You're so pretty, you'd do so well."

"Oh, but I don't even know the show," protested Sharon.

"It's Shakespeare, three scenes from Shakespeare. I could find you a costume—you wouldn't have to speak lines—"

"This is flattering, but I must say no," said Sharon firmly.

Thunstone was on his feet, too. "We expect to enjoy the performance."

"I hope it will go off well," said Grizel Fian. "There are some good effects—the sets, the lights, certain dramatic emphases. Well, thank you for talking to me."

She winnowed away. Sharon rose from her own chair.

"Good-looking, isn't she?"

"Very," said Thunstone, "but not as good-looking as you. Let's go now, hear my friend Reuben Manco."

They met Manco in the lobby. Again he wore his beaded hunting shirt, and in his headband he had stuck an eagle feather, which stood erect like an exclamation point. It was tufted with red at the top, and on the white expanse below the dark upper end were strange devices, also in red.

"You're looking at a medicine plume," said Manco. "It was given to me by John Blackfeather, of the Oglalla Sioux. He told me that it was once worn by Red Cloud, the great chief of his tribe, and that it's a strong charm against evil magic. You two are going to listen to my sermon this morning? Come on, then."

The three went out into bright sunlight, crossed the street on to the campus, and approached Whitney Auditorium. People thronged in at the door. Lee Pitt greeted them at the head of an aisle inside.

"I'll introduce you, Chief Manco," he said, "and then I'll get clear off stage and leave you to massacre the palefaces. You're going to have another full house, it seems. Countess Monteseco, Mr. Thunstone, find yourselves seats."

He went away with Manco. Sharon and Thunstone found

42   THE SCHOOL OF DARKNESS

places on the aisle well to the front. Father Bundren came and stood there. "May I?" he asked.

"Please do," said Thunstone, and he and Sharon moved in to let Father Bundren sit down. "Where's Shimada?" Thunstone asked.

"I don't know. I'd expected him to be here."

All around them rose a buzz of chattering voices from the waiting crowd. The auditorium was filling up fast. Toward the rear sat Grizel Fian, vivid in that red dress she wore. Among a press of people at the back, Thunstone made out a bald head and bulky shoulders, oppressively familiar to him.

He glanced at his watch. It was exactly one o'clock. Lee Pitt and Reuben Manco came on stage, side by side. A lectern had been set there, with a lamp and a microphone upon it. Pitt came close to the lectern. His amplified voice rose in the chamber.

"Welcome, ladies and gentlemen, to the morning session of the American Folklore Survey Symposium," he said. "It's my great privilege to present Chief Reuben Manco of the Cherokee Nation, Master of Arts and Phi Beta Kappa at Dartmouth. Some of you heard him briefly yesterday. Here he is, to speak about what Native Americans have done and said and believed."

With that, Pitt walked away into the wings. Manco came to the lectern and bowed his feathered head to the applause. His brown face had deep furrows, made into dark lines by the overhead lights.

"How," he said, in the deep voice he used for formalities. "Yes, as you've heard, I'm a *Tsukali*—what white men call a Cherokee. I'm a full-blooded American Indian, and I'm proud to say that."

He leaned above the lectern. "Can't many of you claim some of that blood? Genealogists will tell you that if your ancestry goes back before the Revolutionary War, you're

THE SCHOOL OF DARKNESS

almost sure to have Indian blood in your veins. And if your forefathers came here later than the Revolution, by way of Ellis Island, your America is still Indian America. You smoke tobacco, lie in hammocks, eat corn and squash and sweet potatoes, you paddle canoes and wear moccasins and catch American fish and hunt American deer. You are of America, though you forget what America was when the first white explorers found it."

He sighed deeply. The amplifying microphone carried his sigh over the listeners like a lingering puff of wind.

"The white strangers came and took the land from the Indians. They changed everything. Once the buffalo blackened the Western prairies, the passenger pigeons filled the skies with the thunder of their wings. Where have they gone? Where has everything gone? The forests cut down, the lakes and rivers poisoned, the earth made bare and sterile. The Indians never did that, not in their forty thousand years. The white men have done it in less than five hundred. Yes, but you will say, America is progress. The white men have civilized and educated the Indians. But is that really so? Was the Indian really just a savage?"

"No," said somebody in the midst of the audience. Thunstone wondered who had spoken.

"*No* is the right word," said Manco. "Permit me to quote an illustrious American, a man without whom the United States would have had some difficulty in becoming the United States. I refer to Benjamin Franklin. Here's what he said, and I can quote him by heart: 'Savages we call them, because their manners differ from ours, which we think the perfection of civility; they think the same of theirs.' "

He lifted his head with its tall feather and let his eyes rove over the audience.

"Oh," he said in a voice that suddenly rang, "our lands have been taken, but our names stay on those lands. On states called Massachusetts, Connecticut, Arkansas, Ten-

44   THE SCHOOL OF DARKNESS

nessee, Texas; on rivers like the Mississippi, the Missouri, the Ohio, the Potomac; on towns, on villages, all through the country. You can't wipe those Indian names away!"

Again he paused, and smiled as though in self-deprecation.

"But I didn't come here to moralize," he said, more gently. "There isn't time for me to consider all Indian peoples throughout the nation. I'm a *Tsukali,* a Cherokee, and maybe I should just talk about my own people."

Then he talked about the Cherokees. They had once lived in the Lake Erie country, had quarreled with their kinsmen, the Iroquois, and had migrated to the Appalachian country. Before that, as he quoted scientific opinions, they may have descended from the Mound Builders, whose structures still survive in the Mississippi Valley. Coming into what would in time be called the states of the Eastern South, they had lived and hunted and farmed and built their special culture.

"We didn't live in wigwams, we had comfortable houses with pitched roofs," said Manco. "Our chiefs were wise governors and made just laws and saw that those laws were obeyed. We had the finest of stone tools. We had copper, traded from up in the Great Lakes region from which we had come. When de Soto came through, in 1540, we were hospitable to him, courteous to him, although he killed our warriors. Maybe, if de Soto and the others had waited a few centuries, we'd have developed our own civilization, greater than the Aztecs or the Peruvians. As it is, we were called one of the Civilized Tribes. Education? Sequoyah gave us our own written language. John Ross and Elias Boudinet and Major Ridge were our brilliant chiefs. Then came the Trail of Tears and we were exiled across the Mississippi. I won't go into the details of that infamy. Later in our history, Stand Watie and Tandy Walker were generals in the Confederate Army. Like all Indian tribes, we've been stolen stone-blind by the Americans. It was only in recent years

THE SCHOOL OF DARKNESS   45

that we got the guarantee the Constitution gives to all its citizens, that we could worship our own gods."

He cocked his head and grinned. It was a fierce grin.

"None of the newcomer white settlers on our lands wanted that. They wanted to force their own religion on the Indians. Let me quote to you what Sagoyewacha, chief of the Senecas—the white man's histories call him Red Jacket —what he said to a bullying missionary. Sagoyewacha said, 'You have taken our country but are not satisfied. You want to force your religion upon us,' he said. 'We also have a religion which has been handed down from our fathers. It teaches us to be thankful for all the favors we receive, to love each other and be united.' "

He spread his brown hands above the lectern.

"To be thankful, to love each other and be united—aren't those good, wholesome teachings? We Cherokee have the same lesson from those we worship. From back to our be-ginnings, we have turned in reverence to the sun, the moon, the wind and the rain. We respect all living things. We even respect the rattlesnake. Doesn't it seem very likely that all your own prehistoric ancestors turned in reverence to those same elements?"

Father Bundren muttered something that sounded like "huh."

"My convictions are the ancient ones of my tribe," Manco went on. "Yet, allow me to say that I must respect other religions. I feel that any religion whatever is so good that it is better than no religion at all."

A whisper in the audience. Thunstone, looking back, saw that Grizel Fian sat up straight and nodded her head.

"I have knelt down in churches," said Manco. "I believe that my oath sworn on the Bible will bind me. I'm always ready to hear and respect any profession of faith, and I hope you'll hear mine."

He elaborated. He told of the Cherokee belief, not only in

46 THE SCHOOL OF DARKNESS

benificent deities, but in stealthy evil beings. He described the *anisgina,* the grisly creatures that are not ghosts exactly, but things that move and flit like shadows and look for wickedness to do for wickedness' sake. He spoke of the terrible Raven Mockers, the eaters of human flesh, whose arms are feathered like wings to make a roar in the air as they swoop down on a sick or wounded man to suck his blood as a vampire sucks blood. He imitated the cry of the Raven Mockers, *kraa-kraa,* and it seemed to fill the auditorium to its high, vaulted roof.

"And do I believe in these terrible things?" he cried. "I do, because I've encountered them. I'm a Cherokee medicine man, and it's my job to keep them from hurting my people. Do I have magic power? Maybe it isn't good taste to show off, but shall I show off here, a little, for the benefit of the skeptics?"

"Yes," said a voice from somewhere in the crowd, a woman's voice. Manco grinned again, white-toothed.

"Very well, ma'am, with your permission I'll try. I ask you to think of what the weather was like when you came here this morning. Bright, wasn't it? A clear blue sky, not a cloud up there, isn't that how it was?"

He stepped away from the lectern and stood straight, his moccasined heels held together, as though he were a soldier at attention. He lifted his arms above his head, close together. His hands bent forward, side by side, toward the audience.

He began to sing, deeply, rhythmically, with words that Thunstone did not know. After a moment, his feet moved. He paced off in a sort of dance, around in a circle and around, singing all the time in rhythm to his steps.

All watched and listened, in a silence so deep that Thunstone could hear Sharon's deep breathing. But suddenly, a prolonged peal of thunder clattered above the auditorium's high roof, a sort of fusillade of sound that greatened into a

THE SCHOOL OF DARKNESS 47

deafening, crackling roar. And up there above them, the loud patter of rain, like myriad galloping hoofs.

Manco dropped his arms and stepped back to the lectern. He leaned to the microphone. He beamed, as though in triumph.

"Rain!" he cried, his voice ringing above the downpour. "Do you doubt that it's rain? Do you think I'm using some sort of hidden sound effect? Go out to the door, some of you, and make sure."

Two men rose and headed up the aisle. Father Bundren left his seat beside Thunstone and went at a swift stride after them. The rain belabored the roof of the auditorium.

"It's raining, all right," shouted the first man at the door. "Raining bucketfuls!"

"And not exactly needed just now," said Manco into his microphone. "I'll bring it to an end. Keep watch at the door, if you please."

Again he raised his arms, but apart this time, in a V. He went into his dance, he sang again. He made a circle, his moccasins shuffling.

Up there on high, the stormy tumult died away, so abruptly and completely that the silence oppressed. Back to the microphone came Manco.

"Look out there again, please," he called, and the men at the door went out and then came back.

"It's clear," shouted Father Bundren's voice. "The sun's out, no clouds in the sky."

He came quickly back to his seat beside Thunstone. He frowned thoughtfully. Manco waited for him to sit down.

"That's just as I expected," said Manco then. "And now, are there questions?" He pointed to a woman who had raised her hand, and she rose.

"How can you explain your method in bringing rain and then stopping it?" ske asked.

"Certainly I can explain," answered Manco, his voice

THE SCHOOL OF DARKNESS

deep in his chest. "I make a certain mystic sign with my arms and hands, I sing a certain song and dance a certain dance. And that brings the rain, and more of the same sends it away. Next question?"

A man rose this time, gaunt and bearded. "Could you teach your rain-making method to me?" he asked.

"Not unless you're of the true Cherokee blood and are apprenticed to learn the art and wisdom of a medicine man," said Manco. "There are other tribes, mostly off in the Southwest, who dance and pray to bring rain. I understand that they, too, are careful about revealing the secret."

Someone else wanted to know how the Cherokee nation had descended from the Mound Builders, and Manco quoted the opinions of archaeologists and spoke of similarities between recovered artifacts from certain mounds and later tools and ornaments among his own people. Another questioner rose to bring up Manco's remark about respect for rattlesnakes. To that, Manco said that respect for poisonous reptiles did not extend to pushing too close to them, and that Cherokee medicine included the use of remedies for snake bite. Other questions on various subjects. One of these by a lady, about Cherokee cooking, Manco answered with a smile as though of relish. At last:

"No more questions?" he asked. "None? Thank you, ladies and gentlemen, for listening with such patience."

He walked off stage, and Lee Pitt came on and spoke into the microphone.

"It's now half past two, more or less," he said. "At three o'clock, we'll hear from Father Mark Bundren, on the history of diabolism and the influence of its belief today. Tonight, at eight o'clock, the Department of Dramatic Arts presents, under direction of Ms. Grizel Fian, a program of scenes from the plays of William Shakespeare that deal with the supernormal. Now, suppose we take a brief recess until three."

THE SCHOOL OF DARKNESS

Everyone rose; everyone began to talk. As Thunstone followed Father Bundren into the aisle, he felt, as he would feel a physical touch, eyes fixed upon him. Someone had turned at the outer door to look, someone with a bald head and a huge, hooked nose above big shoulders.

"Is that someone you know?" Father Bundren asked.

"Yes," said Thunstone. "Yes, it is."

For it was Rowley Thorne. It could be nobody other than Rowley Thorne.

Rowley Thorne, who once had slid away into nothingness before Thunstone's eyes. Rowley Thorne, who now had returned from nothingness, had returned here upon this campus, whose presence was a black threat to Thunstone and to Sharon, Countess Monteseco.

V

"Is that someone you know?" Father Bundren asked again.

"I'm pretty sure it's someone I know," replied Thunstone. "Will you please wait, right here in the aisle, for a few moments? Stay with Father Bundren, Sharon. I'll see you both later."

He walked quickly forward, jostling people without apology. He came out into the vestibule and through that to the outer porch above the steps. Rowley Thorne waited there. For a moment Grizel Fian was in sight, too, but she seemed to hurry away somewhere.

Thorne faced Thunstone. His high skull was bald with a faint sheen, his nose was a beak, and his wide mouth held itself thin and hard.

"All right, here I am," Thorne said. "What now, Thunstone?"

"I've had glimpses of you again and again, ever since I came here," said Thunstone, looking Thorne up and down. They were both big men, more or less of a height, and both of them strongly, muscularly built. Thorne wore a suit of dark, dull cloth, and his neck was swathed in the folds of a black-checked scarf. Above the scarf, his face had cheeks like slabs, a thrusting chin, a colorless mouth, shrouded eyes as hard and gray as gunmetal. The colorless mouth worked slightly.

"If I hadn't wanted you to see me and talk to me, I wouldn't have waited for you," said Thorne. People moved past them and into the open. One or two glanced curiously

THE SCHOOL OF DARKNESS 51

at the two big, stern-faced men. "Let me ask you a plain, civil question, Thunstone," Thorne said after a moment. "What do you think you'll do about my being here?"

"That's a question I don't care to answer," said Thunstone, who at the moment had no answer. "What I'll do depends a great deal on what you do or try to do, because I'm sure you'll try something. But I'm sorry to see you at all. I did have some optimistic notion that you were gone forever, gone into another dimension, or another plane or something like that."

"You turned my helpers against me," Thorne said, in a tone of harsh accusation. "I summoned them, and you drove them back out of this world. And they took me with them."

"They must have kept you for quite a while," said Thunstone in the most casual of manners. "What happened to you, wherever you went?"

"I wouldn't tell you if I knew, and I don't really know," Thorne flung back. "How should I know for certain? It's like a dream, half-forgotten—you'd wonder if it was real time or space. But I was brought back by the prayers of someone to whom I'll always be grateful."

"Prayers?" repeated Thunstone. "Who prayed for you? To what gods?"

"I've come back," grated Thorne, "to this place called Buford." His heavy brows locked themselves in a scowl. "Now," he said, "you'll try to persecute me, won't you? Try to send me back there again."

"Remember that your journey into nowhere was your own doing. You called on a whole battalion of evil names against me. When I was able to banish them, they took you along. I didn't exile you—they did. You ought to find better company to consort with."

"That's as may be," said Throne. "But now, here I am in Buford, listening to the speeches at this symposium. No law

52 THE SCHOOL OF DARKNESS

forbids me to do that. Goodbye for now. I think we'll be seeing each other again."

"I wouldn't doubt it for a minute," said Thunstone.

Thorne turned and fairly ran down the steps outside the auditorium. For all his size, and he was as big as Thunstone, he moved swiftly, surely. He vanished into a passing group of students.

Thunstone stood where he was. Sharon's voice spoke at his side, a hushed, unhappy voice.

"Rowley Thorne," she was saying. "Rowley Thorne's really here."

"You're right, he is," replied Thunstone. "But I'm here, too. He and I have had encounters before this, and so far he's never had the better of any of them."

"We'll be in for trouble," Sharon almost whispered.

"Trouble," repeated Father Bundren at Thunstone's other elbow. "If I've heard correctly about your Rowley Thorne, he more or less delights in causing trouble. Count on me if you think you need me."

"Thanks," said Thunstone. "I'll certainly do that."

They had walked down the steps to the pavement. They could see university buildings on both sides of the street. They walked a few steps farther, and to the left they could see a wide stretch of open space, green with grass and set with huge old trees. In its middle rose a sort of obelisk.

"I wonder what that monument commemorates," said Thunstone.

"I wonder the same thing," said Father Bundren, "but I'd better get back to the auditorium. I'm due to speak, and I hope speak to some purpose, in about ten minutes."

They returned and went inside together. Father Bundren moved purposefully along the aisle toward the stage. Lee Pitt came past him to meet Thunstone.

"I want to invite you to a sort of potluck dinner before

THE SCHOOL OF DARKNESS   53

the Shakespearean performance tonight," he said. "I can't invite all the guests, there won't be enough for everybody."

"I'm afraid that I must have dinner with Countess Monteseco here," said Thunstone.

Pitt looked at her, smiling his admiration. "Bring her along, too. It will be simple, I say—just a big pot of minestrone and some garlic bread. Let me find you in the lobby of the Inn, say a quarter to six. We'll eat early and then go watch Grizel Fian's show."

"That will be a pleasure," said Sharon. "Thank you, Professor."

Pitt went away. Reuben Manco came to join Thunstone and Sharon.

"Might we sit together?" he said. "I looked for Shimada while I was speaking, but I never spotted him. And I can't see him anywhere now."

They found seats. Around them, voices jabbered.

"Why would Shimada want to miss your speech?" Thunstone wondered.

"You'll have to ask him. The mysterious East, you know."

Pitt and Father Bundren were on stage. As Pitt spoke into the microphone, the babble of voices died down. Pitt introduced Father Bundren, who took his place at the lectern. His head bowed for a moment; perhaps he was praying. Then he looked up. His eyes quested over the well-filled auditorium.

"I've been introduced here as a priest of the Roman Catholic Church," he began, "but I won't try to preach a sermon. For some years I've been occupied in the study of world history, particularly in that bracket that deals with diabolism. At present I'm at work on what I hope will be an informative book on the subject. Perhaps some day it will be published and will be found worth inclusion in your fine library here. But while you wait for that, there is already a

54 THE SCHOOL OF DARKNESS

good assortment of books on creepy supernatural subjects in that same library of yours. You'll find, for instance, the works of Father Montague Summers on witchcraft and devil worship, as well as on the werewolf and the vampire. He is tremendously erudite, he quotes authorities in various languages which he expects you to translate for yourself. And he believes implicitly in witches, monsters, magical phenomena and ghosts—indeed, he claims to have seen a ghost. I recommend his books to you."

Again he studied his audience. Sitting beside Thunstone, Manco made notes on a pad of paper. Thunstone saw that he wrote in the Cherokee alphabet.

"Devil worship goes back to prehistoric times," Father Bundren went on. "We find laws against it in the Penta-teuch, the first five books of the Old Testament, at one time ascribed to Moses. Ancient Greece and ancient Rome rec-ognized and feared diabolism. That interesting, perverse worship came in strongly with Gnosticism, almost as the Christian era began. The Twelve Apostles opposed it, fought it, not with entire success—Gnosticism still exists here and there. But when you're told that there was bloody persecution of witch belief and witch organization from the beginning of the Church—that's an oversimplification, and a false one."

He waited for his words to sink in. Thunstone and Sharon listened silently. Manco continued to take notes.

"As a matter of demonstrable historical fact," Father Bundren said, "the early Church fathers preached against witchcraft for centuries without advocating stern reprisals. The first papal bull launched against witchcraft was that of Pope Alexander the Fourth, in 1258. That was followed by a series of campaigns against the belief, in which I don't know how many thousands of accused witches were exe-cuted, in various untidy fashions. The last Pope to make a clear condemnation was Urban the Eighth, in 1631. But

THE SCHOOL OF DARKNESS

witches were accused and tried and condemned for many years after that, by both Catholic and Protestant courts. In these enlightened times, we recognize that many were found guilty who were only demented or deceived or just driven to confession by torture. Here in America, twenty accused witches went to trial and punishment in Salem. Maybe some were innocent and were condemned by confused judges of that frontier court, but two or three, anyway, were guilty."

Again he looked around. "Guilty!" he repeated. "Guilty of what? Of transgression against the English law that, of course, prevailed in the American colonies. It made the practice of witchcraft a crime. Two or three, I say behaved in a manner that showed that they believed themselves to be practicing witchcraft. Therefore they were guilty of breaking a law, and the court found them so."

Somewhere in the crowd, Thunstone sensed a flutter, and looked in that direction. It was Grizel Fian, seemingly stirred. She seemed almost to be ready to stand and say something.

"And now," said Father Bundren, "it behooves us to consider another definition, the definition of justice. But I can't offer you any such definition. I find myself harking back to what was said once by an illustrious pagan, Socrates, as quoted in Plato's *Republic*. Years ago, I was impressed enough to commit to memory what Socrates said, and here it is, if any of you would like to note it down."

Another wait. Thunstone saw Manco poise his pen above his pad.

"Socrates was talking with half a dozen friends at the house of Cephalus beside the harbor of Piraeus," said Father Bundren, "and he wound up by saying—and I quote: 'For I know not what justice is, and therefore I am not likely to know whether it is or is not a virtue, nor can I say whether the just man is happy or unhappy.'"

He cocked his head, and smiled. "All right, can anyone

56 THE SCHOOL OF DARKNESS

here do better than Socrates at a definition? We're all caught up in our own culture. It's like being well dressed. A naked savage, in his own eyes and the eyes of his fellow tribesman, is dressed in the height of fashion. As for proper religious observance, see how in India a cult that has been suppressed —Thuggee—that worshiped Kali by committing murders. We all adhere to the precepts of our various religions, if indeed we have any religion. Too bad if we have none. I suppose that any religion—even Thuggee—is better than none at all, but maybe I'm prejudiced because of my profession."

He went on to quote from the Scriptures, and suggest that the reported casting out of devils by Jesus and the apostles might have been miraculous healing of insanity. "But miraculous, nevertheless," he said. As for the rise of witchcraft in the early centuries of the Christian era, he shook his head.

"I've mentioned Gnosticism," he said. "It gives some commentators to argue that diabolism is really a very ancient religion, long in existence before Christianity; and it's true that Gnosticism partakes of ancient Egyptian and Babylonian mysteries, with something of Brahmanism and classic Greek and Roman worship and even bits of the then newly established Christianity—altogether, Gnosticism was one of the most accommodating of beliefs. But let's look into the evidence of what witchcraft really was. I say that it's a grotesque and anarchic burlesque of Christian teaching and ritual."

"No!" cried a woman's voice, loud and shrill, and Father Bundren smiled broadly.

"Does someone disagree with me?" he asked cheerfully. "Who said no? Will the lady please stand up? Does she have special information and experience of witchcraft?"

He waited. Whoever had protested made no move.

"Then let me go on. A witch coven tries to have thirteen

THE SCHOOL OF DARKNESS

members—in derisive imitation of our Lord and his twelve disciples. Witches meet and conduct their masses, which are travesties of true masses. They have, for instance, a communion service, which to me seems fairly unappetizing. I won't go into it here. And so on, and so on. Read about these blasphemous imitations in Kramer and Sprenger, in Guazzo, in Montague Summers, in Wickwar, all the demonologists."

He elaborated, citing cases in both Europe and America, paying special attention to the Salem witchcraft trials. He spoke of enlightenment and tolerant viewpoint in recent times. He read aloud the Act of 1735 by the English Parliament, which set aside the law of James I and abolished the death penalty for witchcraft.

"Execution for witchcraft in Britain had become unfashionable before that," he observed. "The last witch to die there, up in Scotland, went to the gallows in 1772. On the Continent, a last German witch was executed for sorcery in 1775, about the time of the battle of Bunker Hill. And in Poland, a court sentenced two convicted witches to be burned to death in 1793. The English Parliament disallowed punishment for witchcraft in 1824, though being somewhat hard on fortune-tellers here and there. And today—"

He paused for effect.

"Today," he said, "witchcraft or any other belief can be practiced, as long as it doesn't transgress laws against things like murder and obtaining money under false pretense, anywhere in the United States. There are even national organizations of diabolists, that perform their ceremonies in public and have conventions and frequently get into the newspapers." His eyes roamed over the audience. "I have reasons to think that such things occur here, in your town of Buford and on your university campus. I've had a person pointed out to me, a person of considerable renown and some per-

58   THE SCHOOL OF DARKNESS

formance in black magic. He's probably present here among you."

There was a stir in the air as heads turned. Yonder, across the auditorium where Thunstone sat with Sharon and Manco, was Rowley Thorne.

"Let that sum up for me," Father Bundren was saying. "God bless you all. Now, does someone have a question?"

The first to put up a hand and rise was recognizable as the man who called himself Exum Layton. His mouth quivered under his limp mustache. He asked Father Bundren if a devil worshiper was damned in the sight of Christians.

"Nobody is damned, if he honestly repents," replied Father Bundren. "Next question."

This came from a young woman, rising close to where Thunstone and his companions sat. She wore a red-striped blouse and blue jeans, both so snug that they showed every curve of her amply symmetrical figure. Her dark red hair was so tousled that it looked like fur.

"How do you reconcile your claim of liberalism with the traditional policy of your Catholic Church to imprison and torture and kill alleged witches?" she demanded.

"I attribute that to a recognition of realities," replied Father Bundren. "My Church can change attitudes and policies, and has done so again and again. Once the Church authorities bullied Gallileo into denying that the earth moved around the sun; but today the Church agrees that nevertheless it does move. I could multiply instances here, but need I do that?"

"You confess to a confusion about justice and its employment." That was Chancellor Pollock, rising in the very midst of the assembly.

"As I remember, I quoted Socrates to that effect," replied Father Bundren. "What I do is recognize the sense of justice as influenced by this culture or that. Justice alone may vary

THE SCHOOL OF DARKNESS

in its sense, according to whether one thinks it can be carried out by death or imprisonment or other punishment, or otherwise by a verdict of not guilty. Let me suggest that along with a sense of justice should go a sense of fairness and a sense of mercy. Now, the lady there at the left."

"Father," said the woman, rising in her turn, "do you truly believe in exorcism of evil?"

"I believe in exorcism, and I have performed it several times," was the reply.

"Can you site precedent? Actual exorcism?"

"There are lots of accounts," said Father Bundren. "I suppose that the most familiar story of exorcism is about Jesus Christ at Gadara. It's told very circumstantially in the gospels of Matthew, Mark and Luke, and I feel like believing that it took place. A spectacularly crazy man lived among the tombs at Gadara. He wore no clothes, he broke chains with which he was bound, and he vexed and sometimes frightened the citizens. When Jesus asked his name, he said, 'Legion; for we are many.' If we go along with the explanation of psychologists for this poor fellow, we must say that he was schizophrenic in a highly complicated degree. The accounts go on to say that Jesus cast the devils out of him and into a nearby herd of swine, which charged at once off a high cliff and drowned in the water below. Whatever happened, the healing of the man was highly dramatic and successful."

"But how can that story stand up?" persisted the questioner. "What about that big herd of swine? How do you explain it when an article of the Jewish faith is to abstain from eating pork?"

Again Father Bundren smiled. "A considerable body of theological research has established that Gadara was a community mostly of pagans, who would have eaten and relished pork, even as you and I. Next question?"

"Who is the person you mentioned?" yet another woman

60 THE SCHOOL OF DARKNESS

asked. "The one you describe as a performer of black magic?"

"I'll have to be excused from answering that," the priest said.

Others rose to ask questions, of varying degrees of rationality. Father Bundren answered these, and at last drew back from the lectern to allow Pitt to remind the audience once more of the dramatic presentation at eight o'clock. Then everyone rose to depart. Father Bundren left the stage and came along the aisle.

"I couldn't pick out Shimada, either. I felt somewhat neglected by him. Why is he staying away?" He frowned at Thunstone and Manco.

"I can't fathom the mystery of the Japanese mind," offered Manco. "Perhaps he's at the Inn."

The party went out together, along the campus sidewalk and across the street to the Inn. Thunstone saw Sharon to her door, then put the key in his own lock. Entering the room, he shut the door behind him.

At once he saw a sooty black blur on the door's off-white panel. His lips tightened, and he looked closer. The mark was in the form of a print of a broad left hand. Thunstone could see no lines of fingerprints.

He stepped quickly into the bathroom, soaked a washcloth with water, and brought it back. He scrubbed vigorously at the mark. The scrubbing had no perceptible effect.

He returned to drop the washcloth in the basin, then went to pick up his phone and ask to be connected with Father Bundren's room. "Hello," came the priest's voice.

"This is John Thunstone, Father, in Room 312. Could you come and help me with something?"

"I'll be right there."

Thunstone waited. A tap at the door, and he let Father Bundren in. Father Bundren studied the mark on the door, bending close to examine it. Finally he straightened.

THE SCHOOL OF DARKNESS

61

"Will you step out in the hall for a moment?" he asked. "Leave me alone with this?"

Thunstone went, pulled the door shut behind him, and stood outside. He heard a mutter in the room, but could not understand the words. At last the mutter ceased and Father Bundren opened the door. His face looked wan, with tense lines driven into it.

"Come in," he said. "Things will be all right now, I think."

Thunstone entered his room again and looked at the inside of the door. The blotch was gone from the pale paint. He could see no trace of it.

"Thank you, Father," he said. "I called in the right man to help me. How did you manage?"

"With this."

Father Bundren held out his open hand. Upon the palm lay what at first looked like a coin. But it was a medal, of silver so old that it looked leaden, and it was attached to a gold chain. Thunstone studied the thing. A cross was centered upon it, and around the cross were set letters, Roman capitals, seven groups of them, worn but six of them were readable.

Thunstone made them out: CSPB OSSMI   URS NSND SUQL IUB.

"What is it?" he asked.

"A medal of Saint Benedict," replied Father Bundren. "He's remembered as one of the greatest of exorcists. How old this particular medal is I can't certainly say, but you can see for yourself that it is very old indeed. Do those letters mystify you? Each group is made up of the initials of the words of a powerful prayer."

"It certainly banished that mark," said Thunstone.

"Yes, completely." Father Bundren carefully stowed the medal in an inside pocket. "However that mark came here, or whatever it intended against you, it's been defeated. And

THE SCHOOL OF DARKNESS

every evil that is defeated will give you greater strength to defeat others."

He sounded weary and he still looked tense, pale. Thunstone went to pick up his brandy.

"Wouldn't you like a drink?" he asked.

"Thanks, just now I'd be glad for one."

Thunstone poured brandy into two glasses and handed one to Father Bundren. They sat and sipped.

"How fortunate that you had that medal with you just now," said Thunstone.

At last Father Bundren smiled. "My son," he said, "I always have it with me."

VI

When Father Bundren had taken his leave, Thunstone went to his telephone again. His hand shook slightly as he picked it up. He grimaced at his own nervousness, and called the number of Sharon's room.

"Yes," said her soft voice.

"Listen, Sharon, will you come and have a drink with me?"

"A drink in your room, dear?" She seemed to laugh softly. "What if the house detective came, too? If this place has a house detective?"

"I'd let him come, and he could have a drink, too," said Thunstone. "He might be glad for one. But I have something important to tell you. Give me two minutes to bring some ice and then come in."

"As you say."

He went out quickly and to the end of the hall and fetched back a plastic bin of cubes from the ice machine. Returning, he washed the glasses Father Bundren and he had used and poured modest drinks of brandy into both glasses and dropped in ice cubes. The door opened and Sharon came in, smiling.

"Why so conspiratorial?" she asked.

He gave her one of the glasses and they sat down, she in a chair, he on the bed. "You'll need that drink when I tell you," he said earnestly.

"Go ahead and tell me."

He did so, describing the black hand mark that no longer

64 THE SCHOOL OF DARKNESS

showed on the inside of the door, describing what he had seen of Father Bundren's actions in driving it away. Sharon drank brandy and went to examine the door.

"Not a trace," she said. "Not a stain. What must it have been? And who—"

"I nominate Rowley Thorne," broke in Thunstone. "Evil is his business, and we two are his targets here."

"His targets," Sharon repeated. "What will he do to us?"

"We'll keep him from doing anything."

He went to where his suitcase lay open and took out a rectangular case the size of a cigar box. It was of dark leather and had no visible sign of a lid. Thunstone pressed his thumb at the side and the case sprang open, revealing a collection of objects. He took one, an oval that looked to be made of red baked clay, two inches by three. Its edges were bound with streaks of silver. It, too, had to be pressed in a certain way to make it open. From it Thunstone lifted a small silver bell, hardly larger than a thimble. It gave a clear, musical jingle.

"Here," he said, "I want you to have this. Keep it with you always, day and night."

Sharon took it from him and studied it. "What is it? I've never seen such silverwork."

"It was carved from a block, it was never cast or hammered out. It was given me once by a highly holy man, because I'd helped him. Look at the letters on it."

She bent close to look. "Latin," she said. *"Est mea cunctorum terror vox daemoniorum."*

"My voice is the terror of all demons," Thunstone translated. "I used it when Rowley Thorne called up devils against me, and I sent them back where they came from, and they took him along. Now he's been prayed back into this world somehow—with prayers to those same devils, perhaps. I won't mention their names, I doubt if that would be lucky for us. Keep that bell always with you."

THE SCHOOL OF DARKNESS   65

"Won't you need it yourself?" she asked.

"Take it and keep it," he said again, and she put the bell down into her bosom. It spoke as she tucked it in. They finished their drinks.

"Now," said Thunstone, "it's not yet four o'clock. Would you like to walk out and see the campus, maybe see something of the town?"

He picked up his cane and they went out together, down to the lobby and across the street to the campus. They walked past the auditorium and other buildings on both sides of the street, and came to where they could look to a great green rectangle of lawn with huge old trees here and there. Turning left, they paced along another sidewalk, broad and of worn, rosy brick. Students walked past them, in groups, in pairs, singly. Most of these were contrivedly untidy, in patched jeans and patterned shirts. Others seemed dressed almost primly, as though they were on their way to church. A gaunt girl in a robelike garment of dark green bobbed up in front of them and stopped them.

"Thunstone!" she shrilled. "Mr. Thunstone, who knows everything!"

Thunstone gazed at her. The hood of her cape was flung back from a rumpled mass of dull brown hair. Her mouth quivered and squirmed in her round face, as though she felt pain.

"You walk with a cane, like a blind man," she said accusingly. "Where's your tin cup, your dark glasses?"

" 'None so blind as those who think they see,' " he said gently, quoting Matthew Henry's worn aphorism.

She blinked at that. Her eyes were gray, pale and dull.

"So," she said, "you've come here to nose things out, things that aren't any of your business."

"I came here because I was invited to speak," said Thunstone. "As for nosing things out, why not? I've done a lot of that in my time."

66   THE SCHOOL OF DARKNESS

"I'll come and listen to you talk tomorrow," said the girl. "If you're still here."

"I'll be here," promised Thunstone.

"Huh!"

The girl went past them, almost at a run. Sharon watched her go.

"I think she's been taking drugs," said Sharon. "Her eyes looked as if she had."

"Lots of young people take drugs," said Thunstone as they walked on. "Lots of people of all ages, when it comes to that."

In the center of the green expanse rose a sort of obelisk. Thunstone wondered what it commemorated. "Let's go over there," he said.

They walked to the monument. On its base were carved the words:

IN GRATEFUL MEMORY OF
SAMUEL WHITNEY
(1801–1871)
FOUNDER OF WHITNEY COLLEGE
I KNOW NOT WHITHER

Sharon studied the inscription. "What's that quotation?" she wondered.

"It's from the *Rubiyat,*" Thunstone told her. "One of the most daunting verses of that poem which teaches us, life is terrible and so is death, so drink and drink and try to forget."

They returned to the brick walk and came to the edge of the campus. A low wall of rough stones, no higher than a tall man's knee, bordered the edge of things. On the far side ran Main Street, along which Lee Pitt had driven Thunstone the day before. A row of students, men and women, sat on the wall. From hand to hand they passed a roughly rolled cigarette, undoubtedly of marijuana. One young man,

THE SCHOOL OF DARKNESS

scrubby in his faded denim clothes, picked at a guitar, not very musically. He sang, and others to his right and left joined in. Thunstone and Sharon stopped to hear:

> Cummer, go ye before, cummer, go ye;
> Gif ye not go before, cummer, let me . . .

Thunstone led Sharon through a gap in the wall, to where they paused to wait for a traffic light to change.

"That song," Sharon half whispered. "It sounded strange."

"It's a very old one, and it has some significance in witch-craft," said Thunstone. "We're told that they sang it at North Berwick Church in Scotland, when they concocted a spell to sink King James's ship at sea."

"North Berwick Church," Sharon repeated. "I remember your telling me about that business. And the chief devil at the ceremonies was named Fian."

"Fian," nodded Thunstone. "Yes. And I'm wondering the same thing you're wondering."

The light changed and they crossed to the opposite side-walk. A squat brick post office stood there, a flag at the top of the mast in front. They walked along Main Street, past a restaurant with a sign that said FAST BREAK, past what seemed to be a stationery shop, past another that displayed T-shirts with strange labels on them. Then a bank, and out of it came the young man called Exum Layton, who had questioned Thunstone that morning.

"Mr. Thunstone," he said at once. His limp-mustached face looked drawn and worried. "It's good to see you, sir."

"Tell me something, Mr. Layton," said Thunstone. "Where does Grizel Fian live?"

"Off there." Layton pointed westward with an unsteady hand. "At the edge of the campus there's an old cemetery, and her house is on the far side of that, the only one at that

68   THE SCHOOL OF DARKNESS

point. It's a big house, it has pillars in front. You walk through the cemetery, and you can't miss it."

"There was a woman dwelt by a churchyard," said Sharon, as though to herself, but Layton glanced at her sharply.

"Shakespeare," he said. "That's in Shakespeare somewhere."

"In *The Winter's Tale*," supplied Thunstone. "Little Mamilius starts to tell a story, he promises it will have sprites and goblins in it. But he doesn't get any farther than the opening sentence, about a man who dwelt by a churchyard."

"That play has my favorite stage direction," contributed Sharon. "Exit, pursued by a bear."

If she meant to make the conversation cheerful, she did not succeed. Layton stood facing Thunstone.

"Look," he burst out. "I want to talk to you, Mr. Thunstone, something very important."

"All right, go ahead," Thunstone bade him. "What's on your mind?"

"Not here, not here." Layton's worried eyes darted this way and that. "It would be better if nobody saw us talking."

"Come with us, back to the Inn."

"I'll meet you there."

"Then come up in a few minutes to Room 312."

Layton darted away along the walk. Thunstone and Sharon turned to return across the campus. They had almost reached the Inn before Sharon spoke. "What do you suppose he wants?" she asked.

"I'm anxious to find out. This morning, he got up in the audience to ask me about the Shonokins, were they real or fiction. Maybe that's what he wants to talk about."

They parted at Sharon's door. Thunstone went to his own room and sat down. He waited for perhaps five minutes. Then came a knock outside, so faint that it was like a bird

THE SCHOOL OF DARKNESS

scratching. Thunstone opened the door, and in came Layton.

He still had a pale, pinched look on his face, as though he was dead tired. Father Bundren had looked like that after exorcising the black handprint. The priest, too, had looked tired. Layton sat down limply in a chair, and Thunstone sat on the bed.

"All right," said Thunstone. "What is it?"

"I got here without being followed," Layton mumbled. "At least, I didn't see anybody following me. I came up the stairs, didn't use the elevator. If they knew I was here, somebody would do something—something bad would happen to me."

"What are you trying to say?" Thunstone prodded him.

"You asked me where Grizel Fian lives," said Layton. "You know about her, don't you? All about her?"

"I don't know all about anything," said Thunstone. "I have thoughts about Grizel Fian. Did you come here to help my thoughts along?"

"I came here for help, if you can give me that. I've been into some things here at Buford State that aren't in the catalog of regular courses, and"—he gulped, and his limp mustache stirred—"I want to get out if I can."

"I'm waiting to hear," said Thunstone patiently.

"Maybe I'd better start at the beginning—the beginning of this school." Layton gulped nervously. "Back when there was just a little settlement here, a few houses, there was a set of people who worshipped devils."

"A coven," suggested Thunstone. "I've heard some talk of that. How they did their spells to cure Samuel Whitney, and how he founded the college here."

"Samuel Whitney founded more than that." Again Layton gulped, as though to steady his voice. "He established a special fund—an endowment, you could call it—for those women who prayed his life back into him."

70   THE SCHOOL OF DARKNESS

"Prayed his life back," repeated Thunstone. "To what god did they pray? To what gods?"

Layton's face crumpled unhappily. "I know the names they prayed to, but I won't say them out loud, not here or anywhere. Whitney wanted a sort of study activity here, for those women, and he set aside a big sum of money for it, the income to go to the activity. Well, the trustees of the college wouldn't hear of anything like that—said it wasn't a proper study course—so Whitney just left the endowment independently of the college, and assigned its income to those who had helped him. You won't find anything about this in any history of Buford State, but I know about it."

"How did he manage his endowment?" asked Thunstone, trying to sit easily, to speak casually.

"The mayor of Buford was named Chunn Emdyke. His wife was one of the group who'd prayed Samuel Whitney back to life. Whitney gave him that money to invest as a trust fund, with the income to go to those witch women."

"I see," nodded Thunstone, who was beginning to see. "And the money from this trust, it still goes on."

"Grizel Fian manages it today," said Layton unhappily. "By now, that fund is bigger than ever. It's grown in the bank where it's kept. Grizel Fian directs it, and directs her followers."

"I've heard that there are at least two covens here in Buford," Thunstone said.

"More than that," said Layton. "I've belonged, Mr. Thunstone." He leaned forward in his chair, tense-bodied, his eyes wide and staring. "I still belong, do you see?"

"How did you get into it?" Thunstone asked him, still calmly.

"Well, I was brought up in this town, all through grade school and high school. I'd heard rumors and whispers—no more than that. But then my parents were killed in an auto accident, and I was an orphan. Grizel Fian looked me up,

THE SCHOOL OF DARKNESS

talked to me, then paid my tuition here at Buford State. Told me certain courses to take. And she taught me things herself."

He shuddered to say that.

"She brought you into her organization of witches," said Thunstone.

"Yes. Yes, she did. I was initiated, and given a coven name—they call me Thief of Heaven. She brought me in so far and so deep that I'm scared." Layton gestured shakily. "The point is, that now she means killing!" he almost screamed.

"Keep your voice down," said Thunstone. "Killing whom?"

"You."

"Me," said Thunstone. "What about the others who have come here? Father Bundren and Reuben Manco and Professor Shimada?"

"This meeting gave her the notion," said Layton. "It's you she's after. Those others, if she can scare them, make them run, it'll be a victory. But you—"

"Will I be a sacrifice, perhaps?"

"That's it, and it will bring her the power to come into the open here—found her own school, call it her own college, make this place a big headquarters for teaching her science!"

"Just like that?" said Thunstone, smiling. "How will she kill me?"

"She can kill and not be caught, she's done it in the past." Again Layton's face squirmed. "But killing you and frightening the others away will dispose of four enemies to what she does and plans. And I don't want to be mixed up in your killing."

"Neither do I," said Thunstone easily. "I don't plan to be killed."

"I'm scared, I say," Layton fairly squealed. "I want out."

72   THE SCHOOL OF DARKNESS

"Good for you. You seem to think I can help."

"Maybe we can help each other," Layton half babbled. "I've warned you, anyway. They're fixing to do something to you, because you're a danger to them. They want to eliminate the danger."

"Eliminate me, in other words," said Thunstone. "That's been tried before."

"But—Rowley Thorne—"

"I've known Rowley Thorne for some years, and he and I have had our contests," said Thunstone. "I don't remember that he ever had the better of any of them."

"To have seen what they did to bring him back to the world, to here in Buford!" Layton cried. "I was there. Grizel Fian and her helpers, those girls who live at her house and others, they talked and sang and danced, and then there he was! Came out of nothing, like Mephistopheles in *Faust.* I'd had enough of that, just watching. I've come to you for help." He gulped. "First thing, I want to be baptized."

"If you've been baptized once, it's for all time," said Thunstone.

"But I was never baptized," chattered Layton. "Only by the witches, not by the church. I want baptism."

Thunstone shook his head. "I can't do that for you, I'm not a minister. You'd better talk to Father Mark Bundren."

"Would he do it for me?"

"I'd think he'd be glad to."

"If I made a confession to him—"

"He'd hear your confession, I'm sure, and advise you. It happens to be his business."

Layton said no more. He sank back in his chair and bowed his head on his breast. Thunstone took up the telephone and dialed the number of Father Bundren's room.

"This is Thunstone again," he said when the priest answered. "I've troubled you once already today and now I'm troubling you again."

THE SCHOOL OF DARKNESS 73

"No trouble, no trouble at all," came the reply. "What can I do for you?"

"I have a young man with me, his name is Exum Layton. He seems to be in great need of spiritual help. Will you talk to him?"

"Of course I will, send him along."

"Thanks." Thunstone hung up and gave Layton the number of Father Layton's room. "He says he'll see you," Thunstone told Layton.

Layton hesitated. "Will he think this absurd?" he asked.

"Not for a moment."

"And the things I'll tell him—will he tell anybody else?"

"A priest never betrays a confession. Go on and talk to him."

Layton went out, his shoulders hunched nervously. Thunstone loaded a pipe with his mixture of tobacco and herbs and lighted it. He smoked and thought, and now and then he made notes on his pad. Time passed. At last he telephoned Sharon, met her at her door, and went down with her to the lobby.

They had not long to wait before Lee Pitt came to greet them. He wore his brown suit and smiled his creased smile.

"We're all ready for you at home," he said. "Ruth—that's my wife—is eager to meet you and talk to you."

They followed him out to his car. He drove them along a broad street, then along a narrower one, and finally stopped in front of a house of white-painted brick with a broad porch. He ushered them into a hallway and then into a comfortable living room with a sofa and stuffed chairs and bookshelves up to the ceiling. At an inner door appeared a woman with streaks of gray in her dark brown hair and a welcoming smile. Two alert teenage boys stood with her. From beyond them appeared a fluffy black cat, which sat down and studied Thunstone and Sharon with intent yellow eyes.

74 THE SCHOOL OF DARKNESS

"Ruth, this is Countess Monteseco." Pitt made the introductions. "And Mr. Thunstone, the man I've been telling you about. Ruth is my wife, and these are my sons, Sam and Dennis."

Dennis Pitt took a step into the living room. "Countess Monteseco," he said with awe in his voice. But Sharon went to him, took his hand, and said that she was glad to be there. The cat turned and walked into the room behind with a smooth, prowling stride.

"Shall I offer you a drink?" asked Pitt.

"Not for me, thank you," said Sharon.

"Nor for me," said Thunstone. "I drank earlier today."

"Then shall we go in and have dinner?" invited Ruth Pitt. "It's simple, but we hope you'll like it."

They went together into the rear room, where a round dining table was set. They stood at their chairs while Pitt said a brief grace. Then they sat down, all but Ruth Pitt, who went away and fetched back a darkly glazed tureen and then a silver dish with sliced bread.

"Garlic bread," she said, "to go with the minestrone."

Pitt served everyone with big pottery bowls of the minestrone. It was strongly made, with brown, nutty-looking garbanzos and smaller, whiter beans, and lacings of green spinach and chips of carrot, cabbage and onion. Thunstone tasted his and found it excellent. There was also a salad of lettuce, sliced cucumber and tomatoes. Everyone ate and talked. Pitt's two sons joined in the conversation. To Sharon's questions, young Sam said that he hoped to study law someday, though just then he was absorbed in wrestling with his high school team. Dennis, it seemed, wanted to be a writer, perhaps a writer like Ernest Hemingway. Sharon asked Ruth Pitt for the recipe for her minestrone, and got a pen and a crumpled envelope out of her purse to jot down what Ruth Pitt told her. The adults had small goblets of white wine, the two boys glasses of milk.

THE SCHOOL OF DARKNESS

Ruth Pitt brought in a dessert of lemon meringue pie, over which Sharon exclaimed with happy praise. When the dinner was over, Pitt led his guests back to the living room.

"Lee," said his wife, "I don't see how I can be going to that show tonight. Dennis needs me to help with some difficult homework."

"Homework?" said Pitt after her. "What kind?"

"Trigonometry."

"Sooner you than me, I was always in trouble with mathematics."

Ruth Pitt left the sitting room. Pitt motioned Sharon and Thunstone to chairs and took one himself.

"To tell you the facts, Ruth doesn't like Grizel Fian," he said. "She won't say so, but I gather that she thinks that if Madame Grizel moved to some other town, it would be no great loss to Buford society. But before we three go over, let's look at tomorrow's program."

"Professor Shimada is to speak," reminded Thunstone.

"Yes, if we can find him," nodded Pitt. "I haven't seen him all day today. He's due to appear in the afternoon. In the morning, I'm doomed to discuss the jagged subject of the supernatural as an influence on American life and literature, and I don't know who'll want to hear me. Then Shimada in the afternoon, if he can be cornered. Later, some seminars, chaired by visiting folklore professors. And after dinner at night, Mr. Thunstone, you'll wind up everything with whatever you have to say. You'll be the hero, so to speak."

"Ralph Waldo Emerson said that a hero is no braver than an ordinary man but he is brave for five minutes longer," said Thunstone, and Pitt chuckled.

"Emerson was brave for five minutes longer, over and over in his life," he said, "but you'll be a hero for more than five minutes when you get up to speak. Now, is there anything else to puzzle us?"

76 THE SCHOOL OF DARKNESS

"Do you know a student named Exum Layton?" Thunstone asked.

"I've known him fairly well for about six years," replied Pitt. "He's a native of this town, an orphan with money of his own, and he keeps taking this course or that without getting quite enough of the right hours to graduate. He's intelligent, but he's erratic. This semester he's been in my folklore class, and he answers fairly difficult questions and asks fairly puzzling ones. Brings odd books along to quote from—Albertus Magnus, Eliphas Levi, even Aleister Crowley. What about Exum Layton?"

"I'd better tell you what about him," said Thunstone. "Tell you in confidence."

"In confidence," nodded Pitt. "Very well, in confidence."

"This afternoon I met him in town," Thunstone said. "I asked him where Grizel Fian lived, and he told me, but the question upset him. Later he came to my room and told me about sorcery and diabolism in town and on the campus, and swore that Grizel Fian was more or less out for my blood."

"He said that?" said Pitt, scowling. "How does he know such things?"

"He said that he'd been an active member in the covens here, and that he wanted to get out. I turned him over to Father Bundren."

"That was the right thing to do with him, I think," said Pitt soberly. "But getting back to Grizel Fian, just why should she be out for your blood? And how does she hope to get it?"

"She has brought in some interesting help for that." Thunstone decided not to name Rowley Thorne, confidence or no confidence. "I'll try to handle that aspect of the case myself."

"And be brave about it for five minutes longer," Pitt

THE SCHOOL OF DARKNESS

added. "Countess, these things seem to worry you. You take them very much to heart, I think."

"I've told the Countess she should never have come to Buford," said Thunstone.

Pitt crinkled his three-cornered eyes. "Perhaps she felt it was right for her to come," he said. "Now, I don't suppose that we should carry these reports to any university authority. But if Grizel Fian has help on her side, you have allies like Reuben Manco and Father Bundren and, if we can locate him, Professor Shimada."

They talked for a while longer, on various subjects. At last Pitt looked at the watch on his wrist.

"The show starts at eight o'clock sharp," he said, "and let's get there early and find good seats."

VII

The Playmakers Theater, near the lot where Pitt parked his car, was small compared to most buildings Thunstone had seen on the campus. It was a flat-roofed cube of ancient brick with gray stone facings. The entry was a low porch with pillars. Pitt said that once it had been a library, before Buford State University grew big and needed a larger library than that.

They got out of the car. Overhead, a round moon blazed above dark treetops. Sharon gazed toward a shadowed stretch on the far side of the theater. "What's over there?" she asked.

"The old town cemetery," Pitt told her. "There's a newer, bigger one on the edge of town, but there's where old Bufordians are buried."

"I've been told that Grizel Fian lives on the far side of it," remarked Thunstone.

"She does indeed," said Pitt. "Her house is alone there, and it's a big, handsome house. If you walk through the cemetery, you'll come right to its back door. I've never been inside."

A massive, metal-braced door stood open and they went in. Inside stood a girl in a black robe that clung to her curves, with a pointed hood drawn well down over her hair and eyes. To Thunstone she looked like the girl who had sharply questioned Father Bundren. Perhaps she was that girl. She addressed Pitt as "Professor" and handed out program sheets.

THE SCHOOL OF DARKNESS 79

They went past her and into the rear of an auditorium with row upon row of red-cushioned seats, an aisle at the center. At the far end hung a dark red curtain with what must be the emblem of Buford State University. Sharon, Pitt and Thunstone sat down at the end of a row of seats.

Across from them sat Father Bundren, and next to him Reuben Manco. They smiled in recognition, and Father Bundren rose and leaned to speak to Thunstone.

"That young man you and I know," he said, "we had some interesting talk. I hope it was profitable."

"Good," said Thunstone. Plainly Exum Layton was not to be mentioned by name. "Is he here tonight?"

"I advised him to miss the show, and ordered him in a good dinner and said I'd see him later."

Then Layton remained in Father Bundren's room at the Inn, and surely that place would be well protected against evil. Father Bundren sat down again, and Thunstone studied his program. It was a single photocopied sheet:

The Buford Players
present
NIGHT SIDES OF SHAKESPEARE
From THE SECOND PART OF KING HENRY VI:
Act I, Scene 4
From HAMLET, PRINCE OF DENMARK: Act I,
Scenes 1, 4, 5
From MACBETH: Act I, Scenes 1, 4, 5
Produced and Directed by
GRIZEL FIAN

There were no casts of characters, or names of the actors portraying them.

Thunstone tilted his sword cane between his knees and looked at his watch. It was exactly eight o'clock. Even as he noted the time, three thudding taps sounded from beyond the curtain. Talk died down. The houselights dimmed and a

80 THE SCHOOL OF DARKNESS

row of footlights came up. A young man of medium height walked into view before the curtain, folded in the sort of black cloak that is associated with Count Dracula in various plays and films. He spoke in a resonant baritone voice:

> "True, I talk of dreams,
>> Which are the children of an idle brain,
>> Begot of nothing but vain fantasy;
>> Which is as thin of substance as the air,
>> And more inconstant than the wind."

Abruptly he fell silent and headed off to the wings.
"From *Romeo and Juliet,*" whispered Thunstone.
"Mercutio speaking," said Pitt.
The curtain rose rumblingly toward the top of the arch. Music stole from somewhere out of sight, a stealthy music, slow and minor. The light was soft and blue, upon a stage set here and there with flowered shrubs. Upstage rose a wall painted to resemble masonry, with an indented parapet at the top.
A dozen girls danced into view, to the rhythm of the music. All of them were finely proportioned, with very few clothes. Their rounded arms and legs were bare; the upper slopes of their bosoms were visible. Their faces shone pale in the dim light, like night-blooming flowers. Nimbly they danced and postured. They began to sing, and Thunstone had heard the words earlier that day:

> Cummer, go ye before, cummer, go ye;
> Gif ye not go before, cummer, let me . . .

That ancient witch song, dating back to the time of Shakespeare and Elizabeth, perhaps before that. This dance and chorus of witches had never been mentioned in the play. Was this an actual ceremony? Who had said once, that if you witnessed such a ritual and did not protest, you your-

THE SCHOOL OF DARKNESS 81

self were a partaker in it? Thunstone shook his head to banish the thought.

> Gif ye not go before, cummer, let me . . .

They broke off the song and fled offstage to the right, and for a moment left the stage empty behind them. The lights blinked off and then on again for a moment, and others entered at left.

First came stalking a huge, heavy-set man in the black cassock and white bands of a medieval priest. He must have been four inches over six feet, and was massively built even for that height. He beckoned with a mighty hand to bring others into view after him—a much smaller man also robed as a priest, then a buxom woman in the loose-folded dark gown and steeple hat of the traditional witch—Margery Jourdain, of course. Behind her came Bolingbroke, caped in star-spattered black with a snug black cap. The huge priest spoke in gruff tones, identifying himself as Hume:

"Come, my masters," he rumbled. "The duchess, I tell you, expects performance of your performance."

"Master Hume," said Bolingbroke, "we are therefore provided. Will her ladyship behold and hear our exorcisms?"

"Aye," replied Hume, "what else? Fear not her courage."

Bolingbroke directed Hume to mount the parapet and join the Duchess of Gloucester there. Hume flung back his cowl, showing a massive face with a tufty brown beard, and made a quick exit. Bolingbroke then ordered Margery Jourdain to "grovel on the earth" and told the other priest, Southwell, to read. Southwell produced a roll of parchment, spread it out, and began to mutter. Meanwhile, on the parapet above appeared the Duchess, instantly recognizable as Grizel Fian. She wore a splendid dress that gleamed like spun silver, so far down off her shoulders as to reveal a generous part of her bosom with the shadowed valley at its

82 THE SCHOOL OF DARKNESS

center. Hume joined her, towering a head above her, but by no means detracting from the attention she skillfully focused upon herself.

She spoke clearly: "Well said, my masters, and welcome all. To this gear the sooner the better."

And Bolingbroke:

"Deep night, dark night, the silent of the night,
 The time of night when Troy was set on fire;
 The time when screech-owls cry, and ban-dogs howl,
 And spirits walk, and ghosts break up their graves,
 That time best fits the work we have in hand."

The priest called Southwark peered at his parchment. *"Conjuro te,"* he began, and then some indistinct words, while Bolingbroke rummaged in a pouch and cast a handful of powder upon the stage at his feet. Thunder rolled loudly, the lights blinked and blinked for flashes of lightning. A pallid blaze sprang up from the powder; a spotlight stabbed its beam down to reveal a figure there.

"Rowley Thorne," whispered Thunstone, and that was who it was, recognizable for all in a cowl-like headdress and a sort of tunic that seemed made of black bearskin. The fire died down and glimmered around his feet as he rose erect. *"Adsum,"* he pronounced.

Still sprawled on the boards, Margery Jourdain bade him answer questions: "For till thou speak thou shalt not pass from hence."

Thorne's deep voice agreed: "Ask what thou wilt."

Bolingbroke then put the questions, and Thorne as the spirit made answers, while Southwark scribbled. King Henry? Henry would die. The Duke of Suffolk? By water would he die. The Duke of Somerset? Let him shun castles. At last: "Have done, for more I hardly can endure."

Bolingbroke again: "Doomed to darkness and the burning lake, false fiend, avoid!"

THE SCHOOL OF DARKNESS 83

Again a deafening roll as of thunder, a glare of lightning, and Thorne vanished before their eyes. The curtain fell and the house lights came up. Thunstone and Sharon and Pitt looked at each other.

"They cut that scene short, before York and Buckingham could show up and arrest everybody," remarked Pitt.

"Because they want to give us the witch dance and the spirit raising, but no reprisals," said Thunstone.

"What did you think of the performance?"

"Fairly impressive," said Thunstone. "That prophesying spirit was Rowley Thorne."

Pitt blinked his eyes. "He's here?"

"I spoke to him on the campus earlier today."

"What's he doing here?"

"I intend to find out."

Bumping, rolling noises behind the curtain showed that scenery was being shifted. The row of lights gleamed, and the young man in the cape walked on behind them. All hushed to hear him as he recited:

" 'Tis now the very witching time of night,
   When churchyards yawn and hell itself breathes out
   Contagion to this world."

Again he made a swift exit.

"But we had that speech, just now," said Sharon.

"No, this is from Hamlet, with Hamlet saying it," Thunstone said.

Up went the curtain on a grim stretch of a fortress with a gloomy battlement upstage. Again blue light for a night scene, with a sky of stars. Francisco and Bernardo came on and spoke of the cold, then Horatio and Marcellus entered, in Elizabethan doublets and hose and cloaks. As they spoke, the Ghost came silently into view. It wore dull gray chain mail and a close-fitting helmet with the visor up.

Horatio addressed the apparition, in the familiar terms of

84 THE SCHOOL OF DARKNESS

wonder and dread, until a remarkably lifelike cock crow sounded offstage and the Ghost seemed to fade away. Horatio and the others felt that it was the image of Denmark's dead king, and agreed to tell Prince Hamlet of what they had seen. A blink-off of the lights and then they shone blue again, and Hamlet was there, with Horatio and Marcellus.

"Hamlet's ahead of time with his suit of sables," muttered Pitt; and indeed, Hamlet wore black doublet and hose, with a mantle of the same color. The three talked about how cold it was, how it was midnight. Hamlet spoke of his father's successor, King Claudius, just then happy among drinking companions. And the Ghost entered again.

The suit of mail was not dull now. By some trick of lighting, and a clever one, it glowed like starlit ice.

"Look, my lord, it comes!" exclaimed Horatio, and Hamlet recognized the Ghost as his dead father. It beckoned him sweepingly and moved away. When Horatio and Marcellus tried to keep Hamlet from following, he fairly roared his threat—"By heaven, I'll make a ghost of him that lets me!" —then fairly raced after the Ghost. Horatio commented, rather darkly: "He waxes desperate with imagination," and after he and Marcellus had spoken briefly to each other, the two of them moved after Hamlet.

The stage blacked out for a moment, and when the lights came up, there was a change in the scenery. A dark wall had been put into place upstage and the Ghost stood upon it, still glittering in its mail. Hamlet gestured to it from below, and spoke: "Whither wilt thou lead me? Speak, I'll go no further."

"Mark me," intoned the Ghost richly, and Thunstone felt sure that this was the same actor who had appeared before the curtain to introduce the scenes. If so, he must have hurried into his chain mail. Hamlet replied, and was addressed again, until the Ghost told him, "I am thy father's spirit, doomed for a certain term to walk the night, and for

THE SCHOOL OF DARKNESS 85

the day confined to fast in fire, till the foul crimes done to my days of nature are burnt and purged away." And followed with the tale of how his brother Claudius had poisoned him, had assumed the crown of Denmark and had married the widowed queen.

All this was familiar to Thunstone and his companions, and was impressively performed. The Ghost departed. Hamlet met Horatio and Marcellus and swore them to silence on the hilt of his drawn sword. "Swear!" came the voice of the Ghost from below, both musical and chilling. And Hamlet:

> "The time is out of joint; O cursed spite,
> That ever I was born to set it right!"

The curtain came down, the house lights came up, and the applause was tumultuous.

"That was done very well," breathed Sharon. "It froze me to my fingertips."

"Grizel Fian is doing herself proud," said Pitt. He looked across the aisle. "Chief Manco, Father Bundren, how do you like the show so far?"

"Interesting," said Manco. "Some things remind me of stories we Cherokees tell each other."

"I'm always sorry about those sinister priests in *Henry the Sixth,*" added Father Bundren, but he smiled to say it. "One bad priest can hurt the work of twenty good ones, which is why there must be far more than twenty good priests to one bad one."

Yet again the houselights went down and the prolocutor paced into view behind the footlights, wrapped in his Dracula cape.

"There's naught but witches do inhabit here," he proclaimed ringingly, "and therefore 'tis high time that I were hence." And off he strode again.

"That's from *Comedy of Errors* this time," said Pitt, "and

86 THE SCHOOL OF DARKNESS

since we're to have something from *Macbeth,* it should be appropriate."

The curtain rose on a dreary, brush-tufted scene, with yet again blue light on it. Three female figures stood together, three strikingly shapely young women in tattered garments, exhibiting slim bare legs, rounded bare shoulders. Their hair flowed and tossed. One was a honey-hued blonde, one a brunette with thick sooty locks, one with red hair that tumbled and gleamed in the blueness. Thunder snarled; bright lights winked on and off for lightning.

"Where shall we three meet again, in thunder, lightning, or in rain?" asked the blonde.

The others answered, speaking of a battle to be lost and won and a fated meeting with Macbeth.

"Fair is foul and foul is fair," they chanted together, "hover through the fog and filthy air."

They continued, boasting of killing swine, of sinking a ship bound for Aleppo. A drum sounded, and Macbeth and Banquo entered. Banquo spoke of the witches, "So withered and so wild in their attire," though the three were young and pretty enough to be cheerleaders.

"All hail, Macbeth!" cried the blonde. "Hail to thee, thane of Glamis!"

"All hail, Macbeth!" spoke up the brunette. "Hail to thee, thane of Cawdor!"

And the red-haired one: "All hail, Macbeth! That shall be king hereafter!"

Macbeth and Banquo declared their mystifications, and the witches vanished.

The stagelights blinked off briefly, and came on again. A huge pot had been fetched onstage. It stood on what seemed to be a writhing tangle of red and blue flames. Macbeth and Banquo were gone, but the three witches paced around the great pot—going counterclockwise, widdershins, Thunstone noted, the traditional direction of a witch circle. Their bare

THE SCHOOL OF DARKNESS

arms wove in and out as they seemed to cast things in. The blond witch chanted, "Round about the cauldron go; in the poisoned entrails throw." Together they sang, "Double, double, toil and trouble; fire burn and cauldron bubble."

Pacing, the brunette witch took up the catalog of the repellant formula. Again the chorus of "Double, double," and the red-haired one went on with the naming of highly unappetizing items. Finally, the brunette: "Cool it with a baboon's blood, then the charm is firm and good."

A blinding flash of lightning, and Hecate had appeared, as though out of the floor. She was singularly fearsome, with three masks glowering to front and right and left, a headdress of snakes that stirred, a robe of wet-looking green and black, and six white arms that moved in singularly life-like fashion.

"O! well done! I commend your pains, and every one shall share i' the gains."

That was the voice of Grizel Fian, Thunstone knew at once. The witches again moved widdershins around the cauldron, intoning a song of "black spirits." Then, said the brunette: "By the pricking of my thumbs, something wicked this way comes."

It was Macbeth who came, to accost the witches. Thunder pealed again, and a head in a helmet hovered into sight above the steaming cauldron. Rowley Thorne's head, and no visible body. "Macbeth! Macbeth! Macbeth!" Thorne mouthed. "Beware Macduff, beware the Thane of Fife. Dismiss me. Enough."

With that, the head was gone. Stage effects were impressive here, thought Thunstone. Another apparition sprang into view above the cauldron, a child or a dwarf streaming with redness as with blood. "Be bloody and resolute," it harangued Macbeth, and vanished in turn. In its place rose another dwarfed figure, wearing a crown and holding aloft a leafy branch of a tree. It uttered its prophecy: "Macbeth

88 THE SCHOOL OF DARKNESS

shall never vanquished be until great Birnam wood to high Dunsinane hall shall come against him." Winding up its speech, it, too vanished, and the entering procession of kings, with Banquo's ghost escorting them, seemed fairly anticlimactic. The curtain went down, but the houselights stayed dim. Someone entered before the curtain. This time it was Grizel Fian, her hideous Hecate makeup discarded. She wore the low-cut silver gown of the Duchess of Gloucester in the first scene presented. She spoke, rhythmically:

> ". . . These our actors,
> As I foretold you, were all spirits, and
> Are melted into air, into thin air;
> And, like the baseless fabric of this vision,
> The cloud-capped towers, the gorgeous palaces,
> The solemn temples, the great globe itself,
> Yes, all which it inherit, shall dissolve,
> And like the insubstantial pageant faded,
> Leave not a rack behind. . . ."

She bowed, and walked away out of sight.

"What did you think?" Pitt asked Thunstone.

"Well done, especially some of the stage effects," Thunstone replied.

"What were they trying to prove?" Pitt prodded.

"That will take some finding out."

Father Bundren and Manco met them in the aisle, and the whole group went out together.

"Did you enjoy it?" Pitt asked Manco.

"I recognized some elements that struck me as subtle, not to say sneaky," said the medicine man. "I said a prayer for strength to my gods. Father Bundren crossed himself twice, which I took to mean that he was saying his own prayers."

"You were right, Chief," said Father Bundren. "It seemed to me that, out of three excerpts from Shakespeare, we were watching what amounted to witch ceremonies. Some of the

THE SCHOOL OF DARKNESS

classicists of my faith say that to be present at such things without making a protest amounts to joining in with them. That's why I prayed."

"Something of the same thought occurred to me independently," said Thunstone. "Professor Pitt, will you be so kind as to take the Countess and my two friends back to the Inn? I'll say goodnight to all of you right here."

"Where will you be going?" asked Sharon quickly.

"Into the cemetery yonder, to begin with."

"Wagh," said Manco. "Let me come along."

But Thunstone shook his head vigorously. "No, let me play the lone hand. I know what I'm doing. You and Father Bundren see the Countess to her door, will you please? Make sure it's all right for her to be in her room."

"We'll be glad to," Father Bundren assured him.

Thunstone looked down into Sharon's face. "I'll call at your door as soon as I get back," he promised.

"As soon as you get back," she repeated. "I'll wait up."

"I'll get back," he said. "Depend on that."

Goodnights were said. Sharon pressed Thunstone's hand and followed the others to where Pitt's car was parked. Thunstone stood among departing members of the audience and watched as the car backed around and went rolling away.

Then he headed for where the cemetery waited darkly under the moon. He swung his sword cane lightly as he walked.

VIII

Somebody came from the theater and paused beside Thunstone. It was the shapely, red-haired girl he had seen at the auditorium, in the lobby of the theater, on the stage as one of Macbeth's three witches.

"You don't believe in our power," she said accusingly.

He leaned lightly on his cane. "I think you have power."

"Come along with me now and you'll be convinced."

She did not wait for him to agree or decline, but walked quickly ahead. Thunstone let her go for perhaps fifty yards, then followed as quietly as he could. His feet fell lightly for so big a man. Up there ahead, in a treeless stretch where the moonlight came down like gleaming rain, was a low stone wall like the one that bounded the campus at Main Street. The red-haired girl walked through a gap in it. Thunstone stood and watched her go in among the murky shadows of the cemetery trees, then followed again.

The path that led through the gap in the wall was strewn with gravel that crunched softly under his feet. Grass grew thickly to either side, and tombstones with rounded tops stood there. They looked like pallid mushrooms springing up from the turf among the trees. Here and there were larger stones, mostly square. Thunstone moved off the noisy gravel and walked on the grass for the sake of silence.

A clear voice rose in a hailing call behind Thunstone. He slid away into the sheltering dark of some low-hanging branches, just as the girl up ahead turned, then came hurrying back along the path. Her feet made more noise than

THE SCHOOL OF DARKNESS

91

Thunstone's. Two more girls came to meet her, almost opposite the point where Thunstone had gone into hiding. Moonlight filtered down upon them and he saw that they were the other two witches of the Macbeth sequence, the blonde and the brunette.

"There's plenty of time yet," one of them said. "Let's go there together."

They headed deeper into the cemetery. Thunstone followed cautiously, still keeping on the grass beside the gravel and under the shadows of the branches.

The three girls talked, not in loud gossipy fashion but stealthily and in undertones. Thunstone could hear their voices but could not make out the words. The journey went on, perhaps for two hundred yards. Once the trio stopped and turned to look back. For a worried moment, Thunstone thought they had seen him or perhaps had divined his presence, but then they walked on again, and he followed them.

They turned from the gravel path into a sort of clearing where the light of the moon was brilliant on the grass. There stood a square, flat-roofed structure the size of a one-car garage. The moonlight was gray upon it, as upon polished granite. A dark door showed at the front. The girls approached and one of them took hold of some sort of catch and manipulated it for a moment, then pulled the door open. Another turned on a flashlight. They went in, and the door closed gratingly behind them.

Thunstone waited behind a dark cedar tree. Slowly he counted to twenty. Then he stepped out into the moonlit open and approached the tomb. He moved swiftly and silently, every sense awake. Something fluttered down, almost touching his head, then slid away in the air. It was a dark, winged something, too big for any bat he had ever seen. Some sort of night bird, probably. Or was it?

He reached the door of the tomb. A granite slab was sunk there, like a doorstep. Above the door were the big raised letters of a name, EMDYKE. Of course, this was the tomb of that long-ago mayor of Buford, the mayor whose wife had ministered magically to help cure Samuel Whitney. And the tomb was an entry to—something, somewhere.

The door itself was a grating of upright iron bars, set close together. Each bar was as thick as Thunstone's sinewy wrist.

He felt for the catch and tried to lift it, but it hung stubbornly in its place. He exerted his considerable strength, with no success whatever. It was caught and locked; it could be opened only by a special pressure. He tried yet again. The catch did not move.

He bent closer in the moonlight to study the massive framework of the door. Sure enough, a keyhole showed beneath the catch, a slot blacker than the black iron. He twisted the handle of his cane, freed the silver blade, and set the keen point in the slot. Carefully he probed. He twisted this way and that. He heard a muffled clank within the big lock, and when he took hold of the catch again, the barred door creaked on its hinges and swung slowly outward.

At once he was inside and pulled the door after him. He heard the grating of the lock as it engaged. For a moment he stood against a wall of stone, waiting for his eyes to become more used to the gloom.

Some radiance from the moon filtered in between the close-set bars of the door. He could see something of the chamber into which he had come. Against each of the walls to left and right was set a chestlike structure, of stone like the tomb itself. He went to one, felt it. There were raised letters upon it, a name or perhaps an epitaph, but he could not read them by groping. The broad slab of the lid above had a massive padlock. It felt rusty.

He sought the other sarcophagus and found a rusty padlock there, too. "Probably just as well," he said under his breath.

THE SCHOOL OF DARKNESS

For these two stone coffins must hold the bodies of Mayor Emdyke, who had sponsored the witches of Buford, and his wife, who was one of those witches.

He resheathed the blade in his cane and slid the ferrule across the stone floor. He found his way to the rear of the crypt, and there his cane encountered a drop downward.

Kneeling, he explored with his fingers. Here were stairs, leading into the earth, into a deep blackness. He rose, felt ahead of him with his cane, and began to descend. He moved his feet carefully from stone step to stone step, making sure of position at each move. He counted twelve steps going down. Then he was on a broad, roughly flagged floor, in darkness just less black than ink.

He peered ahead of him. His right hand encountered a rough wall, and his cane, held out straight in his left, touched a wall opposite. That meant the width of the place was perhaps nine feet. He extended the cane above his head, to touch some kind of ceiling. Another nine feet, as he estimated.

He began to move ahead. His left hand slid his cane back and forth on the stones in front of him, questing the way like the cane of a blind man. His right hand kept his fingertips to the stone wall beside him. He paced ahead and ahead. He was in some sort of passage, beneath the ground of the cemetery. It would lead him somewhere. Where? That was what he had come here to find out.

Up there ahead, the darkness seemed to fade ever so slightly. The fingers of his right hand on the wall told him that the passage curved, ever so gradually, little by little. He was making a slight turn, and up ahead might even be some sort of visibility. Step by step he accomplished. The light to the front grew more apparent, more, until it seemed a rosy glimmer, like a sunset on a dusty day.

Again he was making a slight curve on the way he went, this time leftward. The passage made a slight S as he fol-

94 THE SCHOOL OF DARKNESS

lowed it. More steps, and then he could see fairly well. There ahead of him was the rose-tinted light, and he saw that it filtered through some sort of a curtain there ahead, a curtain of translucent red fabric. Against it was outlined a blotchy shadow, as though someone stood inside it on watch.

As Thunstone established these things, he heard a soft flutter of sound in the corridor behind him, heard muffled voices. More people were coming in. Whatever he did, he must do fast.

He moved rapidly in the rose light now, and as he moved he stooped and picked up a handful of pebbly stuff. He came close to the curtain at one side, and hurled his pebbles with all his strength to where it came down at the far edge. It patterned there like rain, and the shadowy form behind the curtain half said an oath and moved quickly in the direction of the noise. A head pushed out at that edge of the fabric, even as Thunstone slid past the edge near himself and into something like a granite-faced vestibule. Swiftly he stole to where a carved obelisk stood near the inward wall, and slid behind it.

He must be in a sort of basement. Manifestly it would be Grizel Fian's basement, for he had been told hers was the only house at the edge of the cemetery.

Feet scraped outside the curtain and a man's voice cried out, *"Sapht!"*

The guard inside drew the curtain open. Peeping cautiously, Thunstone saw that that guard was a gaunt man in a robe with the hood flung back.

"Come in, come in," he invited gruffly. "But why all the noise?"

"Why not all the noise?" returned the man who had spoken the countersign. "We're here, and there'll be noise enough."

Eight or ten had entered. Thunstone could see that most

THE SCHOOL OF DARKNESS

were female. They trooped away past the obelisk and through a roughly made arch into somewhere beyond. Bringing up the rear was a towering, broad male figure in a cassock. Undoubtedly he was the actor who had played Hume in the first scene of Grizel Fian's presentation.

Thunstone stayed in hiding and stealthily watched until the guard turned his face back to the red curtain. Then, swift and soundless as a night-prowling cat, Thunstone moved to the archway and through it. As he did so, he heard a drum begin to beat somewhere, a slow rhythm. He moved toward that sound, and wondered where he was going.

So often in the past, he had gone somewhere without knowing where. That was what he did now. It was what he had chosen to do with his life. Now again, he must follow an unknown way he had chosen. Nor could he lose his life, no matter what Grizel Fian planned to do to him.

He came into another passage, lighted this time with iron-bracketed oil lamps fastened to the slaty gray walls on either side. Those were old, old lamps. Undoubtedly they could be considered as valuable antiques. *Pom pom pom* sounded the rhythmic beat of the drum. The passage made an abrupt turn to the right. Thunstone crowded close to the wall at the left as he followed the turn. He saw another archway, with drapes of deep purple cloth drawn to either side. Above the sound of the drum he heard a sound of muttering voices, surely the people who had gone there ahead of him. He stole gingerly to one of the hangings, slid in among its ample folds, and peeped out into what was beyond.

That was a great chamber, long enough and wide enough for a ballroom. It must be the whole basement of Grizel Fian's house. More purple fabric covered the walls, and into the hangings, designs had been worked in black and gold. If these were letters, they were not Greek or Arabic; they were

96 THE SCHOOL OF DARKNESS

of no alphabet Thunstone knew. The spacious floor was paved with something as pale and smooth as wax. At its center was painted, in blue and red and yellow, a design of a great five-pointed star, girded round with a black circle. The spaces between the points of the star were adorned with grotesque figures, and all around the outside of the circle were strung more of the letters that were neither Greek nor Arabic. Thunstone knew a pentacle when he saw one, and he knew that a pentacle was for the focusing of dark, supernormal forces.

Oil lamps hung from the ceiling, shedding their radiance. At the far end of the floor stood a great thronelike chair of dark, polished wood, with a cushion as red as fresh blood. In the gloom behind it seemed to be a flight of stairs. Beside the throne stood a blue-robed man, pounding on a kettledrum. A little to his rear stood two more blue-robed figures, another man and a woman. And ranged along the walls to right and left stood others, the two lines of them facing each other across the pale floor with its pentacle.

There were forty or so of them, as Thunstone estimated. Most of them were young women, but here and there stood men. One of these was the giant who had played Hume in the first scene at the theater that night. He still wore his priest's cassock, but his stage makeup had been wiped off. He bulked huge there, a full head taller than the girls on either side of him. The drum thudded, thudded.

Other music joined in, strange wailing music. The man beside the drummer played a fiddle, the woman blew on some sort of flute. As these instruments blended into their harmony, a figure moved out of the shadows behind the throne and into view. It was a female figure; it was Grizel Fian, in the low-cut gown of silvery cloth she had worn on the stage. The music fell silent.

"Awake, strong Holaha!" cried Grizel Fian in a voice like a bugle.

THE SCHOOL OF DARKNESS 97

"Holaha!" repeated the two ranks of listeners.

"Powerful Eabon!" repeated Grizel Fian. "Athe, Stoch, Sada, Erohye!"

Again the chorus repeated the names. Those were names that Thunstone knew, names he had heard invoked by his enemies in the past. The lamps glittered and blinked, seemed to cast a gory light. A sort of dimness, like gray fog, crept in the great chamber. The air seemed heavy. Thunstone clutched his sword cane closely, felt a quiver from its handle. The silver blade within the cane was aware of where it was. It responded. It made itself ready.

"NOW!" blared Grizel Fian at the top of her ringing voice. "The time is now—the past is gone, it is not! The future has not come, it is not! NOW, NOW, is our moment."

"NOW!" her hearers fairly bellowed in response.

"Rejoice, rejoice," Grizel Fian cried to them. "We seek and worship the one true wisdom, given us by the great ruler on earth, as he was in heaven!"

"AMIN!" chorused the listeners.

As he was in heaven, Thunstone repeated to himself. Lucifer, son of the morning, had ruled in heaven, had been cast down from heaven. Lucifer was the god these people worshiped.

Thunstone, cautiously peering from the folds that hid him, saw those listeners sway and writhe where they stood. Grizel Fian had caught them up into the wild show she was giving them. Again her voice, even more loud and commanding:

"Here, here, in the dark away from unbelievers, we are shone upon with the light of wisdom!"

And light sprang out, greater, more glaring light than the flickering lamps could give. An impressive trick, if indeed it was a trick. Grizel Fian gestured widely with both bare arms.

98 THE SCHOOL OF DARKNESS

"Wine now, to pledge one to another, drink!"

From somewhere appeared two scurrying girls, their loose dark hair tossing snakily, their bodies hidden only by little scraps of cloth. Each carried a brown jug in one hand, a bundle of goblets in the other. Swiftly they passed the goblets out, swiftly they splashed wine into them, and Grizel Fian's followers drank greedily, with wordless cries of relish. Grizel chattered out something, words that sounded like a burlesque of the communion service. At last:

"Dance now!" she commanded them, her arms lifted again. The air was heavy; it seemed to hold cloudy mist that made the lights of the lamps dance.

"Dance now!" she called again, and Thunstone saw the listeners fairly ripping off their clothes, the robes they wore, the shirts and jeans they wore. Their naked bodies glistened weirdly. They moved toward the center of the floor and formed a new arrangement of themselves. Around the pentacle ranged a circle of them, two by two. All the men were in that circle, each with a girl for a partner. Unkempt hair tossed; bodies quivered. Around this circle formed another, a wider one. The music of drum and flute and fiddle rose again. Insinuatingly minor. The two circles began to dance.

"Haa, haa!" cried a girl.

"Sabbat, sabbat!" responded a man's deep grumble.

"Dance here, dance there!" cried Grizel Fian.

The paired dancers of the inner circle trod a measure, turning their backs to each other. The outer dancers paced more slowly, around and around to the left—counterclockwise, the classic widdershins of dancing witches. The couples laughed and jabbered incoherently. As they danced, the men fondled the naked bodies of their partners. Thunstone saw the giant who had played Hume, wearing only a pair of big, clumsy-looking shoes. His mighty chest and arms were matted with tangled brown hair. He picked up his girl and almost fluttered her in the air above him. His muscles flexed

THE SCHOOL OF DARKNESS

and swelled—plainly he spent hours at work with weights. Effortlessly he tossed the girl high in the air. She shrieked, from startled terror or crazy joy. His bearded face grinned as he caught her, put her on her feet again, and danced on with her, not missing a step.

"Now he comes among us!" Grizel Fian shouted. "He, the advocate, the ambassador of our lord in the lowest!"

As she spoke, she caught the top of her silver dress with both hands and dragged it down below her waist, stepped out of it, and flung it to the floor. She stood revealed, palely shimmering in the misty light. She wore only what seemed like the skimpiest of bikini panties, sewn all over with jewels, red and green and yellow and glittering white. Standing with arms lifted, she flaunted her full breasts as the giant in the throng flaunted his hairy muscles. Seldom, Thunstone realized, had he seen such a fine figure of a woman, or one so blatantly, vainly displayed.

"Are we all present?" she cried.

"Not Thief of Heaven, he hasn't come," replied the girl with red hair. "He wasn't at the theater, he isn't here."

"His excuse for absence had better be a good one," declared Grizel Fian bleakly. "If he has disobeyed a command, we have no use for disobedience, for any kind of failure. But nevertheless—"

A pause. Thief of Heaven, Thunstone remembered, was Exum Layton's coven name. All gazed at Grizel Fian. Well they might—she postured like a star of a burlesque show.

"He comes!" she cried again, and dropped to her knees and bowed toward the throne. Silence in the misty hall.

Somebody, something was descending those shadowed stairs behind. A burly figure emerged into the clouded light. It wore a purple robe that hung to the floor, and on its head was set a pair of curved horns, like the shape of a murky crescent moon. But Thunstone instantly recognized Rowley Thorne.

100 THE SCHOOL OF DARKNESS

"Here," rumbled Thorne. "Here we deal with our enemy. He mustn't last out this night."

"Amin," shouted the big man, and "Amin, amin," echoed the others. Their voices echoed in the great chamber. They had gathered in a huddled throng in their nakedness.

Grizel Fian had risen to her feet again. She lifted her bare arms. "Hear the sentence," her voice rang out. "Hear the manner of execution."

"Amin!"

"Bring out the image," Thorne was ordering, and Grizel darted out of sight behind the throne. She was back in a moment. Across her ivory shoulder she seemed to bear a great, limp body in dark trousers and jacket. This she flung down at Thorne's feet. It lay face up, a dummy that seemed made of pillows dressed in clothes. The pallid face bore a painted black mustache, and a tangle of black yarn showed for hair. It sprawled on the floor; it looked limp and helpless there. All the naked watchers stared. But none of them seemed so naked as Grizel Fian. She postured. She knew what she was doing.

On sandaled feet Thorne paced to the throne and sat down upon it.

"Our enemy's time is come," he rumbled.

"Amin, amin," agreed the watchers. Their voices echoed back and forth from walls and ceiling.

Grizel Fian had risen to her feet again. She flung up her arms. "The altar, the altar," she chanted. "Set the altar."

Half a dozen of the group dashed away behind the throne and came back with two stout wooden trestles and a dark rectangle of some sort of stone, the size of a door. They set the trestles before the throne, clear of the prone dummy, and hoisted the slab upon it. Thorne pointed his finger at Grizel Fian, who came and lay upon the makeshift altar, face up. Her body glimmered. Thorne rose and came for-

THE SCHOOL OF DARKNESS 101

ward. Stooping, he kissed her bare belly, then he moved a foot to trace a cross on the floor.

Then this was going to be the mass of Saint Secaire. Many had wondered who Saint Secaire was. Thunstone had read, in an obscure notation to a book about diabolism, that some identified him with Saint Caesarius of Arles, who in the fifth century had been a stern enough enemy to devil worshipers. At any rate, the mass that bore his name was a singularly blasphemous one. And here it was to be performed.

Thorne stood before the altar and the supine body of Grizel Fian and mouthed some sort of ritual, hard to understand. He waved his hands, and the onlookers began to recite in unison:

"Ever and forever, glory the and power and . . ."

The Lord's Prayer, recited backward. As Father Bundren had said, these ceremonies were mockeries of orthodox masses. At last Thorne stepped away from the improvised altar and motioned to Grizel Fian, who rose quickly and moved to a place beside the throne.

"And now to our enemy," proclaimed Thorne.

Grizel Fian flung up her arms again. She writhed and quivered.

"Hear the sentence," she chanted. "Hear what his fate will be."

"Amin!" they all responded.

"The image to the altar," commanded Thorne, and Grizel stooped, lifted the dummy, and flung it upon the altar slab where she had lain. It slumped there, face up.

"The likeness of our enemy," growled Thorne. "John Thunstone. Deal with him, Grizel, you have the right, you have the method."

"He will die," she said. "His allies, that priest-creature, that Indian savage, can read the message of his finish, will flee in terror. The other one, the smirking Japanese pedant

102 THE SCHOOL OF DARKNESS

—he seems to have retreated already, he must have seen what the future holds here."

That meant Shimada. If she was right, if Shimada had fled, then Shimada was not on her side. But where had he gone?

"Amin!" again.

"But Thunstone," cried Grizel Fian, "he who is so certain of his strength, who rests tonight in his room yonder, he is doomed."

"Amin!"

The music began again, drum and violin and flute. Grizel darted back behind the throne, returned with a spear in each hand. The hafts of the spears were as shiny black as charcoal. Their heads gleamed redly, like copper. Stooping beside the altar with the sprawled effigy, she laid one spear on the floor. Its head pointed past the throne where Thorne sat. She stooped lower, as though to sight, and moved the spear a trifle. Then she straightened again, the other spear in her right hand.

"There," she said, "we point our spell to where he lies. And the midnight hour comes when his fate will close on him."

She faced the gathering and lifted the spear to the full length of her arm. She chanted, naming names Thunstone knew from the past:

"Haade . . . Mikaded . . . Rakeben . . . Rika . . . Ritalica . . . Taarith . . . Modeca . . . Rabert . . . Tuth . . . Tumeh . . ."

And high over her head she flourished the spear. Its copper point shimmered in the lamplight. Her whole body waved like a flag.

"I have made my wish before," she intoned. "I make it now, and there never was a day in which my wish was not granted."

THE SCHOOL OF DARKNESS 103

"No use in striking that dummy!" Thunstone cried at the top of his voice.

Every head turned toward him. He came out from where he hid in the drapery and strode swiftly into view, his silver blade drawn.

"It's not going to work," he shouted. "You haven't pointed your curse to me in the right place. Here I am, and I'm come to stop you."

IX

Thunstone had stunned them, every one of them, by his sudden rushing appearance. They stood like uncouth statues, flat-footed, with goggling eyes and wide-open mouths as he came charging across the floor, across the gaudy pentagram. In his right hand he poised his unsheathed silver blade with its prayer inscription, while in his left he carried the sheath of the cane. Naked bodies, male and female, sagged out of his way to the left and the right. Even the hairy giant who had played Hume lurched clear of him. Perhaps they thought he was part of the ritual Thorne and Grizel Fian were creating.

At a dead run he went among them and through them to where Thorne sat staring in his strange regalia, to the altar where the slack effigy lay limp, to where Grizel Fian stood and shakily poised her copper-headed spear to strike downward.

With a powerful, whirling motion of his arm, Thunstone circled his silver point around that crude dummy of himself. He felt a tingle in his right hand as he did so; he heard a singing whine as of a plucked banjo string.

"Now go ahead," he grinned at Grizel Fian. "Stab at it."

Her eyes flamed at him. Her lips writhed apart to show him her clenched teeth. Her naked body flexed itself quiveringly. With all the strength of her arms she darted her point at the effigy.

A frantic, quivering rattle of sound, and the spear's shaft shattered in her hand at midstroke. The copper head

THE SCHOOL OF DARKNESS
105

skipped and sparkled across the floor. Grizel Fian stared at the splintered end of the shaft in her hand, then she hurled it at Thunstone with deadly intent. He batted it away with the shank of the cane in his left hand. It flew clear of him, to clap and clatter on the pale paving.

"Too bad," he mocked her at the top of his voice. "Too bad, isn't it?" he threw at Rowley Thorne, who still had not moved from where he sat and stared mutely. "Things aren't turning out the way you planned, are they? You have to have helpless targets. Let's see what I can do here for a change. I'm not helpless at all."

He made a sudden slash at the grotesque dummy of himself. The cloth of its dark jacket ripped and some sort of cottony stuffing leaped out of the pillow inside. The shape stirred where it slumped. Thunstone shoved at the stone slab with his elbow, shoved powerfully. The slab tipped off the trestles and spilled the dummy to the floor. It fell in an awkward heap. He laughed aloud at everyone in the chamber.

"No harm to me, you see?" he mocked. "No harm whatever. You were pointing to find me and strike me at a place where I didn't happen to be waiting to be found and stricken. Pick up that other spear, somebody. Try again."

Thorne found his voice at last. "What are you doing, standing there like fools?" he blared at the frozen onlookers. "Come on, capture him. We'll deal with him, here and now!"

There was a stir in the naked assembly, but not a bold one. Thunstone stepped clear of the overturned altar and the dummy. He whipped his blade around him in a whistling circle, pivoting on his feet as he did so. He knew that he postured, even as Grizel Fian had postured.

"Didn't you hear what your master said?" he called out derisively. "Come on and try to cross that line I drew—any

106 THE SCHOOL OF DARKNESS

of you, all of you." Again he turned to face toward Thorne and Grizel Fian. He smiled bitterly at them.

"Your mumbo jumbo has gone flat, hasn't it?" he jeered. "Somebody or other isn't listening to you, not very closely. I'm afraid that I've embarrassed you, breaking in on you like this, all uninvited. Shouldn't I remove myself, wouldn't my room be better here than my company?"

"You stay right where you are," shrilled Grizel Fian.

She bent and snatched up the other spear, the one she had positioned on the floor to point toward the Inn, where she had expected Thunstone to be a target for attack. She poised it above her head as though either to thrust or to throw.

Thunstone made a long, smooth stride toward her with his right foot. He slashed powerfully with his blade, and heard it sing in the air. The head of the spear went in a jangling somersault across the floor.

"And now what?" he challenged her. "Shouldn't I just get out of here, I say, and leave you to your jabberings?"

"Capture him, I told you!" Thorne howled, surging to his feet.

Thunstone moved swiftly to make his way around the throne and toward the dim stairs. The musicians had fled to huddle in a corner. For a brief moment Grizel Fian stood to oppose him, her mouth open and trembling, her eyes staring, her bare body drawn up. Thunstone extended his arm. The keen point of his blade almost touched her between her stirring breasts.

"I'd really hate to," he said to her, "but I will if I have to."

Her cheeks went pale as milk and she cowered aside. Thunstone darted behind the throne in the same instant. He made out those darkened stairs, wide, thick slabs of old brown wood. They must lead somewhere upward to ground level. He sprang upon them and went racing up, two steps at a time.

THE SCHOOL OF DARKNESS 107

"I said, bring him back!" Thorne's voice came roaring. "I give you the power to do that!"

Thunstone heard the sudden stamp of pursuing feet.

The stairway was dark, but at the top of it showed cracks of light around a closed door. Thunstone got to that door even as those feet mounted the stairs below him. He groped for a knob, turned it, and ran into a lighted room with high shelves of dark-bound books and a table on which stood a crystal globe the size of a small melon. On the far side was another door, of sooty-black wood with metal clamps. Thunstone rushed at that, dragged it open, and sprang out upon flagstones in the white light of the great soaring moon.

Before him stretched a shadowed expanse of clumps and shrubs, a garden of what plants he could not see, could not wait to see. At the far side of it rose a tall, shaggy hedge. Thunstone made for that, hoping that there would be no rails or wire fencing to stop him, and he drove through a twining of thorny branches, his strong body smashing its way. Then he was out in the cemetery again, with its tombstones and trees. He heard the chirping voices of tree frogs, of night insects. He ran on into the open, and behind him sounded the rattling struggle of his pursuers as they came through the hedge after him.

He snatched a backward look as he dodged between bone-pale gravestones with rounded tops. Three shapes followed him there, their naked skins shiny in the moonlight. One was the huge, hairy man who had played Hume. He dwarfed his companions. For a moment the three halted, close together, as though they peered and searched. Then one cried out hoarsely and pointed to where Thunstone went. Again they followed. He could hear the fall of their feet.

He had always hated to run from anything. He ducked into a clump of leafy laurel and waited there, catching his breath. He could hear them talking.

108   THE SCHOOL OF DARKNESS

"Here's where to settle him," said the booming voice of the big man. "Right here in this cemetery, where it's convenient. Let the police come looking for him and find him here. Let them wonder why he died here."

"He's hiding somewhere," said another of the three, nasal-voiced.

"He can't hide from us," blustered the giant. "He can run but he can't hide. We'll dig him out and leave him for them to dig under. It'll be a pleasure."

Thunstone felt fury swell within himself and strove to master it. Now, if ever in all his life, he needed a clear, cool head. But he was through with scurrying and skulking like a hunted animal; he had never done those things well. He stepped out into the open and let the moon shine on him. The frogs and the insects had fallen silent.

"But how now, Sir John Hume!" he said, quoting a line of Shakespeare. "Seal up your lips, and give no words but mum."

The huge bearded face lifted. Its eyes blinked in the light. "It's you, huh?"

"Who else?" Thunstone flung back at him. "Didn't you come out here looking for me? All right, here I am."

"Quoting from that play, are you?"

"It seemed appropriate," said Thunstone. "The way you feel that this graveyard is an appropriate setting for what we might do here."

He fell on guard with his blade. A moonbeam flickered on it.

The big fellow swayed forward a heavy pace and then another, like an elephant. He looked immense in the moonglow. His shoulders were like great ledges. The matted hair crawled on his broad chest, his thick arms, as he flexed his muscles. His body seemed to spread, like the hood of a cobra. The whites of his staring eyes glittered.

"You think you've got some kind of charm in that trick

THE SCHOOL OF DARKNESS 109

stabber of yours," he said. "It just so happens I've got a charm or two myself. Come on, let's see how quick and easy I can take it away from you."

"Let's see you try," Thunstone invited.

The bulky shape moved forward another ponderous step. The two smaller men advanced from either side, as though to close in on Thunstone's right and left.

"*Kamban-wa,*" came a clear, good-humored voice from somewhere apart from them all. "Good evening."

A small, dark-clad figure stepped delicately into the moonlight to stand at Thunstone's left. A toothy smile and a pair of spectacles sparkled.

"Who in hell is that?" roared the giant.

"*Kudashi,*" said the newcomer silkily, and his voice was the voice of Tashiro Shimada. "Please, Mr. Thunstone, let me attend to this matter."

The great hairy figure edged forward again, and Shimada seemed to flash to close quarters. There was a scrambling blur of limbs. Thunstone heard a wild yell as of pain. He saw the great hulk of the giant body whirl up against the stars of night, then fall clumsily and heavily. Tashiro Shimada stepped over the man he had felled and faced the one beyond.

"You, too?" he inquired, as though offering hospitality.

That man exclaimed as he turned and ran crazily, off into shadows toward the hedge. The other faced Thunstone for a moment. Thunstone slid into a lunge and flicked out his point horizontally, then shifted and brought it down vertically. The moonlight showed a slashed cross on the man's cheek. A wordless cry and that man, too, whirled and fled away. Only the Hume giant lay where he had been thrown, writhing and whimpering on the grass. Shimada stooped and studied him, then straightened again.

"He's not badly injured," he reported casually, "though he will be very sore and repentant tomorrow."

110 · THE SCHOOL OF DARKNESS

"How—" began Thunstone as he brought out a handkerchief to wipe the point of his blade.

"Only judo," said Shimada, coming back toward him. "Our ancient Japanese system of self-defense, in these days rather supplemented by karate. I have always been fairly good at it, though never one of the black belt masters. But this big overgrown man will ache all over when he comes to himself. Come, Mr. Thunstone, let's be tactful and go away."

Thunstone sheathed his blade in the shank of the cane. He and Shimada turned from the fallen giant and walked off among the graves. They came out upon the graveled path that Thunstone had seen before, in silence. Finally:

"All of us have wondered where you disappeared to," said Thunstone.

"Have you? So sorry if I caused you any concern. But I was extremely busy, extremely."

The frogs and insects were singing again.

"Busy with what?" Thunstone asked.

"With Shinto," said Shimada. "With what it can say to illuminate the seeker."

They walked together on the crunching gravel. Thunstone began to realize that his night's adventure had made him tired in muscles all through his big body. He had thought himself in fine phsyical condition, but he had been through strenuous adventures.

"See," said Shimada, his slender finger pointing. "That tomb. The tomb of Emdyke the long-ago mayor of the town, who as they say was friendly with Buford's witch ladies. But Shinto tells that he was more than just that. He used witchcraft himself to gain possessions, to wield power to his profit. He was what you Americans call a wrong guy."

"I'm not surprised to hear it," said Thunstone, "but I'm surprised that you were out here tonight."

THE SCHOOL OF DARKNESS 111

"Shinto again. It helped with the knowledge that you came to Emdyke's tomb and went inside, and on to what you found beyond, at the home of Grizel Fian."

Shimada had come close to Thunstone as he spoke, and a tangy odor smote Thunstone's nostrils. "Cedar," he said. "I smell cedar."

"Yes, cedars grow in this cemetery. I took the precaution of rubbing cedar needles on my face and hands, of putting twigs in my pockets, for possible help."

"The Japanese do that?" asked Thunstone.

"No, but I heard of it from Reuben Manco, as used among his Cherokee tribesmen. I decided to be eclectic, to take any advantage."

Thunstone stood a moment to look at the Emdyke tomb. Again some huge flying thing flapped wings above them. He wondered again how that Hume giant fared, if he still lay where Shimada had so heavily thrown him. They walked on toward the campus.

"What does Shinto say to the worshiper?" Thunstone asked.

"Oh," said Shimada. "Shinto says—Shinto has forever said that there is life and knowledge in every moment of every existing thing. Not only in the animals and plants, but in everything."

"I've heard that much," said Thunstone, swinging his cane.

"In everything," repeated Shimada, as though to emphasize the point. "In rocks, from as big as a mountain to as small as a pebble. In wells, in rivers, in oceans and in little ponds no larger than pools. In empty, deserted houses— very strongly in those—and in tombs and in the bones of the dead, like the bones of Mayor Emdyke back there. In all things, I say, everywhere, all the time, all times."

Walking, Shimada stared pensively up at the stars on the velvet cloak of the sky.

112 THE SCHOOL OF DARKNESS

"Shinto means the way of the gods, more or less," he went on. "It must have always meant that, all the way back to the first men in Japan, those men who chipped stone for tools, who were finding out how to think and speak. As I said today in the auditorium, the Japanese people are two hundred thousand years old or more. I think that Shinto is as old as the Japanese. It is not a late importation like, say, Buddhism, or, more recently, Methodism or Congregationalism."

As he talked, they approached the low wall with its gap that marked the boundary of the campus. Beyond rose the Playmakers Theater, where Grizel Fian had staged her bits of Shakespearean witchcraft and ghostly visitation. The theater was unlighted now, silent now. They passed through the gap in the wall.

"How does Shinto come into these things you've been doing?" was Thunstone's next question.

"From my first moments here, I sensed a strangeness of things at this place, as you did," said Shimada. "Sensed it as you did, as Reuben Manco and Father Bundren did. But I myself am not a good enough Shintoist. I fear that I've become a sophisticate, even an Occidentalist, in some ways. And so I made inquiries here and there, and on the campus I met a very, very good Shintoist indeed."

"Who?" asked Thunstone.

"He is a student here on some sort of international fellowship. His name is Oishi Kyoki, and his Shintoism is by long inheritance. His father in Japan is a distinguished scholar and mystic, has spent his life in the study and perfection of Shinto, and he has taught his son very well. Oishi Kyoki listened to my worried questions and agreed to help and went into communication."

"What communication?"

"At first with trees, with stone walls," said Shimada as they walked past the theater. "Then he established a sensa-

THE SCHOOL OF DARKNESS 113

tion of hearing Grizel Fian herself—what strange books she read, what dishes she handled as she ate. Those objects spoke to him, and he heard. It was a profound experience for me to witness."

"I can imagine," said Thunstone, who did imagine vividly. "What was your result?"

They followed a concrete walk away from the theater toward the center of the campus.

"I have said that I'm not as good at Shinto as Oishi is. I watched and listened. Sometimes I could assist. And tonight we learned what Grizel Fian did, what you did. We followed you almost to her house tonight. We heard how you embarrassed those devil worshipers. We were in the cemetery and saw you face those three men who hunted you, saw you about to be attacked. Then I waved Oishi away and made bold to help. As of now, our side is very much ahead in the game."

Thunstone nodded agreement as they walked. "I'd like to meet your friend Oishi Kyoki," he said.

"Well, perhaps later. Perhaps tomorrow."

It was late. No traffic. No traffic moved on the street as they crossed and entered the Inn. A couple of guests, a man and a woman, sat in stuffed chairs and seemed to doze. The clerk at the desk read a book.

"You've done amazing things, Professor," said Thunstone. "More than I've done toward solving an ugly thing."

"But you ventured your safety, your life," Shimada said. "I only watched and waited."

"You watched and waited, and you knew what you were doing every moment," insisted Thunstone. "Professor, I think the Japanese will rule the world someday."

Shimada's teeth flashed in a smile.

"But of course," he agreed smoothly.

The elevator purred to a stop and the door slid open. They stepped in.

114   THE SCHOOL OF DARKNESS

"Would you come to my room and have a drink?" Thunstone.

"I would be honored."

Thunstone pressed the button for the third floor. The elevator took them up and they emerged into the corridor.

"Let me check here before we have that drink," said Thunstone. "I promised that I would."

He knocked at Sharon's door, and listened. No movement inside. He knocked again. "Sharon?" he called. And no answer.

"Sharon!" he cried, more loudly. He grabbed the doorknob and wrenched and rattled it. Silence. He turned to the watching Shimada.

"She's not there," he said, and surged his shoulder against the door. It creaked, but it did not give.

"Here," said Shimada, "shall we open it?"

In his hand was a plastic credit card. Carefully he inserted it at the lock of the door. He manipulated judiciously, a hand on the knob. Then he drew the door open. The room was alight, and Thunstone went quickly in.

Sharon was nowhere in that room. He saw that the door of the bathroom was open, and that just inside lay a blue silk robe. He hurried to see, dropping his cane on the floor. She was not in the bathroom, either. The window was open, perhaps a foot.

"She's gone," he said to Shimada, coming back. He looked at the bureau. Upon it lay her cross with its gold chain, and beside the cross was the little silver bell he had given her.

"She's gone," he said again, and he knew how stupid he sounded.

Shimada stooped and picked up a folded paper from the carpet. "For you," he said, handing it to Thunstone.

THE SCHOOL OF DARKNESS 115

On the outside was written in pencil, in a bold, sweeping hand:

Please give this to my friend
JOHN THUNSTONE

X

Thunstone opened the paper. He took one glance, and his brows locked into a scowl. "Look," he said to Shimada. "Look at this."

Shimada came to his side. Together they read:

My Dear Thunstone:

On the outside of this letter I spoke of you as my friend; because now my old hope for friendship with you seems about to bear rewarding fruit. This message comes to you by telekinesis—a term beloved by the late great Professor Charles Richet—movement of solid objects across distances. It is to inform you that I hold a delectable hostage, someone you prize highly. If you hope to see her again, you must come to mutually profitable terms with me. Needs must when the devil drives, says the old proverb, and just now the devil is solidly in the driver's seat.

We were ill-advised to try to kill you earlier tonight, and how glad I am that things have turned out like this. Getting hold of your Countess was no great problem, once I gave my attention to it and employed methods. I am able to see great distances when I have a mind to, and to perform great feats. I came to the street just opposite her window. When she laid aside the talismans you had given her—had, indeed, laid aside everything—to take a bath, I had only to say certain words and to beckon, and there she was outside with me, unclad and utterly mystified. I put her into the car I

THE SCHOOL OF DARKNESS 117

had brought along, and now she is safely sequestered, in small, comfortable quarters. Not, let me hasten to say, with Grizel. No point in bringing police or others to search Grizel's home. I have my own establishment, and you don't know where it is.

So now, to be abrupt, what are you going to do about it? Helpfully I suggest that you be calm, be practical, that you come to a good agreement with me. I've fought you in the past. Tonight, as I've confessed, I was in a mood to destroy you, and I've admitted that that was spiteful. Never have I underestimated you, and since like all living things I have complexities and contradictions, I've never utterly disliked you.

So here, my new friend and ally, is what I would say you must do. To begin with, don't talk tomorrow at that meeting. Make an excuse, you can come up with a good one. Meet instead with me, at a place I'll choose. It should take very little time for us to decide what to do in a mutually rewarding relationship. One thing is to exert pressure to found and advance a whole department of interesting studies and experiments here at this Buford State University. Your influence would make this operation a success, and you must exert that influence, impress the university authorities, win them. I couldn't, but you can. But before that, dismiss those other tiresome visitors here, that priest, that Oriental, that Cherokee posturer. Let them go back to their own world, the limited one that recognizes no more senses than five, no more dimensions than three. But you stay here, help me, and receive back your enchanting Countess.

And if you say an angry no? Well, then you'll never see her again. If we can't have you, we'll keep her instead. She might not be as great a help as you, but she can be of some use, having known you so long and

THE SCHOOL OF DARKNESS

well, having seen some of your methods. If you renounce her to us, we'll take time and trouble with her. Eventually, she will join us. She will come to despise you for abandoning her. And she should be a great pleasure to associate with. She is so beautiful.

Suppose then, that I call you on the telephone at about sunrise, and hear what you have to say to this, if anything.

With great admiration and optimistic expectation, I am

> Your future partner,
> Rowley Thorne

Thunstone cursed aloud and almost tore the letter. Shimada took it from him.

"Now," said Shimada, "this is a time to be utterly rational."

"Yes, you're right," agreed Thunstone harshly. "Look, will you go and get Manco and Father Bundren? Bring them to my room, Number 312."

"At once."

Shimada was out of the room, swift as a lizard. Thunstone hurried to his own quarters, dropped Thorne's letter on a chair, and went to his open suitcase. He pawed into it to the bottom, where he had packed books. One of these he brought out, a small volume in a gray paper cover that was worn and tattered. The title was in heavy black letters:

JOHN GEORGE HOHMAN'S
POW-WOWS
or
LONG LOST FRIEND
A collection of Mysterious and Invaluable
Arts and Remedies
Good for Man and Beast

+   +   +

THE SCHOOL OF DARKNESS 119

He opened to the first page, and read the preface he knew by heart:

Whoever carries this book with him, is safe from all his enemies, visible or invisible; and whoever has this book with him cannot die without the Holy Corpse of Jesus Christ, nor drowned in any water, nor burn up in any fire, nor can any unjust sentence be passed upon him. So help me.

He turned more pages, searching for something he seemed to remember, when Shimada came in again. Behind him were Reuben Manco and Father Bundren, and behind Father Bundren entered Exum Layton, limp-mustached, pallid-faced.

"I've brought our friend Layton along, he doesn't care to stay anywhere by himself," said Father Bundren. "Now, what is this story that Professor Shimada has half told us?"

"Read that," said Thunstone, pointing to the letter on the chair.

Manco picked it up, and Father Bundren came to his side. Together they read it, in tense silence.

"Well," said Father Bundren at last, "this Rowley Thorne seems confident, seems full of pride, which we're told goes before a fall. But what's that you're consulting?"

"A book of Pennsylvania Dutch charms and spells. The Long Lost Friend."

"Wait," Father Bundren said quickly. "Isn't that a book of witch enchantments?"

"Not that exactly, as I think," Thunstone said. "John George Hohman came to Pennsylvania early in the nineteenth century as an indentured servant. He worked off his indenture, he became respected for kindliness and help. His book recognizes evil influences, but mostly it's about how to ward those off. Between times, he tells you how to cure sick horses and cattle, how to make molasses and beer and how

120   THE SCHOOL OF DARKNESS

to get rid of mice and rats." He looked fixedly at Father Bundren. "I want to use a charm that's included here. I hope you won't object. I hope you'll help me."

"What charm is that?" It was almost a concession.

Thunstone turned more leaves of the book. "Here it is," he said, "page seventy-eight. It says, 'To Compel a Thief to Return Stolen Goods.'"

"You think it would work?" asked Exum Layton, the first words he had spoken since he had come into the room.

"And why should it not work?" challenged Shimada. "A thief—isn't Rowley Thorne a confessed thief, by what his letter admits? And isn't the Countess stolen goods? She is good. Read the charm out, Mr. Thunstone."

Thunstone did so:

"Walk out early in the morning before sunrise to a juniper tree, and bend it with the left hand toward the rising sun—"

"Junipers grow out there in the parking area," broke in Manco. "I noticed them. And it's early, early morning now, sunrise is hours away. Excuse me, go on. 'Toward the rising sun,' you said."

Thunstone read on:

"—while you are saying, Juniper tree, I shall bend and squeeze thee, until the thief has returned the stolen goods to the place from which he took them. Then you must take a stone and put it on the bush, and under the bush and stone you must place the skull of a malefactor."

He paused: "Here are three crosses marked on the page," he said.

Father Bundren bent to look. "Those must mean the signing of the cross three times. Thunstone, I take back my

THE SCHOOL OF DARKNESS 121

doubts about the worth of this formula. But do you believe it?"

"Yes, I do," said Thunstone promptly. And here's the end of it: 'Yes you must be careful, in case the thief returns the stolen goods, to unloose the bush and replace the stone where it was before.' See here, gentlemen, I've known this spell to work in Pennsylvania. I witnessed it myself."

"I believe that spell, too," spoke up Manco.

"If we all truly believe, it will work," pronounced Father Bundren. "Chief Manco, lead us down to your juniper bush. And let's bring along that *Long Lost Friend* book. We'll follow it's directions to the word."

"But we need the skull of a malefactor," reminded Thunstone.

"I can bring that," said Shimada. "You will be out behind the Inn, you say? Go on down and wait for me there. I'll find you."

He was gone at a swift, scurrying run. When the others came into the hall, he was already out of sight.

They hurried down two flights of stairs, out through the almost-deserted lobby and out into the Inn's parking area, among ranks of silent cars. Manco led the way, and Layton diffidently brought up the rear.

"Does anybody have a flashlight?" asked Manco, and Father Bundren handed him one. Manco turned on the beam and went to where shrubbery grew at the pavement where the parking area came to a border. He quested with the light among various growth, and then said *"Wagh."* He had come to a row of evergreen bushes.

"Here we are," he said, standing above a shaggy specimen about four feet high. In the light of the torch it showed almost as tall as Manco's chin. Its branches were thickly grown in small needles, whorl after whorl of them. Thunstone recognized it as a juniper.

"We need a stone to make it bend down," he said.

122 THE SCHOOL OF DARKNESS

"Here," said Layton. "I've found one that ought to do."

He had been questing here and there among the shrubbery. Now he came back with a stone the size of a loaf of bread. In the light of the torch it showed smooth, with blotches of gray and white.

"Thanks," said Thunstone, taking it to examine.

"Now for that skull of a malefactor that Professor Shimada went to find," said Father Bundren. "We'll have to wait for that."

Manco flicked off the light and handed it back to the priest. They stood silently together and waited. Thunstone burned inside with thoughts of Sharon, with a deep agonized wonder of where she might be, of what could be happening to her. Moments of time crawled past, seemed to join into an eternity. At last, at a very last:

"Here comes somebody," said Father Bundren. "Yes, it's Shimada."

Shimada hastened to them. He held up a pale, round something, something with deep, dark eyeholes, with a row of grinning teeth.

"Whose skull is that?" asked Thunstone.

"We spoke of him earlier tonight," said Shimada. "I got this from the tomb of Mayor Emdyke, who once worshiped the devil. He was certainly a malefactor."

"How did you force the lock of the tomb?" was Thunstone's next question, and Shimada's teeth shone in a smile, shone almost like the teeth of the skull.

"Shinto," he replied, and no more than that.

Manco went back to kneel at the juniper. "Let me have that," he said, and took the skull and set it at the roots of the tree. "Now, what next?"

"Give me the flashlight," said Thunstone, and tucked the stone under his arm and opened the *Long Lost Friend*. Again he read aloud: " 'Bend it with the left hand toward the rising sun—' "

THE SCHOOL OF DARKNESS   123

Father Bundren bent down the juniper toward the east. He whispered something, probably a prayer.

Thunstone went ahead: " 'While you are saying, Juniper tree, I shall bend and squeeze thee, until the thief has returned the stolen goods to the place from which he took them.' "

Father Bundren repeated the words aloud. "And now the stone," he said, still bending the juniper. He took the stone and weighted the branches down. The juniper sagged under the weight.

"And the triple sign of the cross," said Father Bundren. He made the three signs, his hand moving carefully in the light of the electric torch. "And now, to see what happens."

He turned toward Thunstone as he spoke, but Thunstone was off at a headlong run. He sped through the lobby and up the stairs, two stairs at a time, two flights. He almost flung himself at the half-open door of the room from which Sharon had been spirited.

"Sharon!"

"Oh," her voice said, almost too softly to hear. "Oh, yes."

She stood trembling in the middle of the floor, her blue robe huddled upon her. She looked at him, with wide, frightened eyes. Then she ran to him and they were in each other's arms.

"Not so hard, dear, you'll break my ribs," she said. "Oh, thank God, thank God! How did I get back here?"

"I'll tell you all about it in a minute. You're all right, you haven't been hurt?"

"No, but it was such a frightening thing. They got me away to some sort of house on the edge of town—"

"They?" he repeated. "They?"

"It was in a car. Rowley Thorne and Grizel Fian. I don't know where they took me—"

124 THE SCHOOL OF DARKNESS

Father Bundren was at the door. Behind him stared Layton, and with Layton were Shimada and Manco.

"Is all well?" asked Father Bundren breathlessly.

"She's back, and she doesn't seem to have been hurt," replied Thunstone. "The charm was good."

"Because we all had faith," said Father Bundren.

"I had faith," murmured Sharon, still trembling as Thunstone held her. He seated her in a chair. She pulled her robe around her. Through its thin blue showed the pink of her bare body.

"Now that stone must be taken from the juniper," Thunstone reminded. "Must be put back where it came from."

"I'll go do that, I know just where it was before," said Layton, and hurried away.

"And I would do well to return that skull," spoke up Shimada.

"Let me go with you," said Manco, and they departed, too.

"As for me," said Father Bundren, "I'll do some necessary things in the bathroom yonder. Something of what I did to keep evil influences out of your own room, Mr. Thunstone."

He went through the open door. They heard his voice speaking rhythmically in Latin. Sharon sat and held Thunstone by his arm, shuddering as she clung. He put out his other hand to pick up the cross and chain from her bureau.

"Put this on, and keep it on," he said.

"I will." With shaky fingers she fastened it around her neck.

"And here," said Thunstone, taking the silver bell. "Keep this with you, too."

She cuddled the bell in her hand. It chimed faintly, musically.

Father Bundren came back to them. "I've done my best," he said. "I invoked powerful holy names. And I went so far

THE SCHOOL OF DARKNESS

as to trace a cross in ink, on the window sill. If the management complains, I'll pay whatever seems to come under the heading of damages. And you dropped this." He held out Thunstone's cane.

"Thank you," said Thunstone, taking it. He had forgotten all about it.

"And I'll say goodnight," said Father Bundren, smiling. "Good morning, I should say."

He went out closing the door behind him. Thunstone sat on the bed and Sharon came and sat close against him.

"Just what happened?" he asked her.

She drew up her shoulders inside the blue robe. "It was like a dream. An awful one. I suppose I was half unconscious—maybe I was hypnotized. We were in a car that ran along and ran along, somewhere to the edge of town, I think—"

"Which edge of town?"

"I don't know which. I was foggy in my head, I think. But it was a house with trees thick all around it and they got me in—into a room with old brown wood paneling—and put me in a chair. And laughed. Rowley Thorne kept laughing."

Again she shuddered, as though an icy wind had struck her.

"What did he say to you?" demanded Thunstone. "Tell me everything."

"Well—he kept crinkling his eyes and sniggering. And I told you, I was there with nothing on. He talked about how beautiful I was, how he didn't blame you for being dazzled, and how he was dazzled himself. But Grizel Fian—"

"She was there?"

"Yes, she'd been in the car, she'd come into the house. And she didn't like how he acted toward me, and she said so. Her voice got shrill and sharp. But Rowley Thorne laughed at her, too. Told her not to be jealous—told her

126   THE SCHOOL OF DARKNESS

that you'd soon be with them, be one of them. And he said he knew that she was drawn to you, and he'd help her with some kind of a love potion—"

She broke off and covered her face with her hands. Fear was still upon her.

"Did he touch you?" Thunstone asked her. "Did he dare do that?"

"No, he didn't touch me. I don't think that Grizel Fian would have let him. But he said that when the sun came up, everything would be arranged. That you'd be won over to them and you'd help them with some plan about the university here. I was too upset to understand just what they meant. And they offered me some wine, but I wouldn't touch it."

"I'm glad you didn't. All right, what then?"

"Oh, both of them talked and talked. I don't know how long—maybe hours, for all I could tell. Then, all of a sudden, I was back here, picking up my robe and putting it on."

At last she seemed calm again.

"We got you back," Thunstone told her. "Shimada and Manco and Father Bundren helped. We used a charm from this book, this *Long Lost Friend.*" He took it from the pocket of his jacket. "Long lost or not, it came through for us. And you're back safe, and you needn't ever be afraid of Rowley Thorne again." His jaw grew square, his mouth hardened. "I'll see to him before this day's done."

"And now what must I do?" Sharon asked.

"Lie down here on your bed and sleep. You need sleep."

Her hand went to her face again. "I couldn't sleep, I'd be afraid to."

"No," he said, and rose and went to a chair. "I'll sit here and watch while you sleep."

"Oh, will you? Will you stay with me?"

Her tremulous tenseness had quite departed. She drew back the coverlet, lay down, and pulled the coverlet over

THE SCHOOL OF DARKNESS 127

her blue-robed body. Thunstone watched. She was silent. At last she breathed regularly. She slept.

Thunstone took off his jacket and laid it aside, doffed his shoes, loosened his tie and the collar of his shirt. From his cane he drew the silver blade. Stooping, he read again the words upon its flat:

Sic pereant omnes inimici tui, Domine.

He turned off the light in the room. Through the window beat a soft wash of moonglow. He sat down and laid the blade across his knees.

He watched Sharon as she lay there, quiet and trusting and at rest. He himself was dead tired from the adventures he had gone through. He closed his eyes and at last slumber came upon him, too.

XI

Thunstone did not sleep soundly in that chair. Disturbing dreams came, and he wakened again and again, to look at Sharon asleep on the bed. Once he rose and moved silently on shoeless feet to see her closer at hand. She slept quietly, motionlessly; she breathed easily and deeply. She seemed relaxed, trustful. He was glad for that, and returned to his armchair. He drifted off again, and this time no dream came.

When next he opened his eyes, the light of dawn showed at the window. Sharon stood in the room, dressed in a black suit of smooth, rich cloth. Her jacket flared slightly below the waist. Under the jacket she wore a white, stock-collared blouse, gathered under her chin with an ascot knot. Her hair was neatly combed, and she had on makeup. She smiled at him, smiled happily.

"Did you rest well?" she asked. "I tried not to make any noise as I got myself ready to go out. I dressed in the bathroom."

"I'm glad they didn't bewitch you out of it again," said Thunstone, rising.

"But Father Bundren marked a cross on the window sill, and I wore this." She touched the cross at her neck. "And I kept this." She lifted the silver bell, and it faintly pealed. "And I'm all right."

Thunstone pushed his feet into his shoes and took up his jacket. "Come to my room while I get ready for today," he said. "I want you close at hand, every moment."

THE SCHOOL OF DARKNESS 129

"Yes, of course."

They went to Thunstone's quarters, and she sat on a chair. "Here," he said, and handed her the *Long Lost Friend*. "You'll find the spell that got you back on page seventy-eight."

He carried fresh clothes into the bathroom, and quickly showered and shaved and dressed. When he came back, Sharon looked closely at him. He picked up his cane.

"You're a handsome man, and I hope you want your breakfast as much as I want mine," she said as they went out. "Do you suppose we'll see Rowley Thorne downstairs?"

"I hope so," said Thunstone grimly. "I very much want to see him."

They got into the elevator. They were alone in the cage. "What would you do if you met him?" Sharon asked.

"Never mind. I wouldn't tell anybody that."

"Not even me?"

"Especially not you."

She smiled. It was a rather strange smile, faint but soft. "You sound stern," she said, and he did not reply. As they rode down, the walls of the elevator seemed close, seemed almost crowding. Downstairs in the lobby they saw nobody they knew, anywhere, all their way to the dining room.

There, again, Thunstone's eyes probed everywhere for familiar faces. At a table against the far wall sat Exum Layton and a slender young man with a brown face and stiff black hair. Layton saw Thunstone and Sharon, too, and lifted an arm as though to beckon. He and his companion rose as Thunstone led Sharon to the table.

"Good morning," Layton greeted them. He seemed more cheerfully easy than Thunstone had seen him so far. "Let me introduce Mr. Oishi Kyoki. I stayed at his place last night."

Oishi Kyoki bowed ceremoniously to Sharon and gave

130 THE SCHOOL OF DARKNESS

Thunstone his lean brown hand. His face was young and thoughtful; his eyes were creased at the corners. "This is a great honor, sir," he said, in accented English. "Professor Shimada ate breakfast early, very early, but he said I should stay and perhaps meet you. Please sit down with us, both of you."

"Thank you," said Sharon, and took a chair. Thunstone stood for a moment, studying the room and the guests at the table. At last he sat down himself.

"No sign of Thorne, or of Grizel Fian," he said.

"Might they be here in disguise?" Layton wondered apprehensively.

"I think I'd know them, even in disguise," said Thunstone.

"And so, I think, would I," said Kyoki.

A waiter came, and Sharon and Thunstone ordered their breakfasts. Kyoki spoke courteously in answer to questions from Thunstone.

"Mr. Layton here can be confident of safety with me," he said. "No evil can pry and seek and find him where I live."

"How can you defend him against that?" Sharon asked.

"Shinto," smiled Kyoki. "If you know Shinto, it will defend."

"Could you expound Shinto to me?" Thunstone suggested.

"Only if you would truly accept it as the one way to enlightenment."

They talked as they ate. Kyoki repeatedly declared that he was honored to sit in the presence of Thunstone. Layton ventured to say that he was glad to have assisted, even so slightly, in the rescue of Sharon. As he spoke, he admired her with his eyes. When all had finished eating, Thunstone looked at his watch.

"Professor Pitt will speak at ten o'clock," he said. "Shall we go over together?"

THE SCHOOL OF DARKNESS 131

"I have classes with Professor Pitt," said Kyoki. "He is inspiring."

"He's been my advisor," added Layton.

They went out together, across the street and into the auditorium. As they came along the aisle, Father Bundren raised his black-clad arm to call them to him. Manco was there, too, in beaded buckskin shirt and headband. Thunstone and Sharon took seats next to them, while Layton and Kyoki found places directly behind. A moment later, Shimada appeared and sat behind in his turn. Again Thunstone peered this way and that among the occupants of the auditorium, in search of Thorne or Grizel Fian or both, and again he found neither.

"No, Thorne is not here," said Kyoki behind Thunstone, as though he had read Thunstone's thoughts. "I do not know where he is, but he is not here."

"Shinto, I suppose," said Thunstone.

"Yes, Shinto helps me to know."

"And Grizel Fian?"

"She is not here, either. I read her to be in her house, her big house. And she is not very happy there."

Voices died down as Lee Pitt appeared on stage and advanced to the lectern. He adjusted the microphone, and spoke into it.

"Good morning, ladies and gentlemen," he said. "In a program such as ours, now and then comes a terrible moment when the chairman makes a speech. This is that terrible moment." A murmur of laughter, and he waved it away. "I have been directed to say something about the importance of fantasy in the literature of America."

He arranged a paper on the lectern and studied it for a moment.

"Fantasy," he repeated. "Maybe we'd better start by defining the term. We could go along with a dictionary into which I looked before I came here to speak, where it says

132 THE SCHOOL OF DARKNESS

that fantasy is imagination, is the paying of attention to supernatural matters. All right then, fantasy has been with us from the very first known writings of mankind. *The Odyssey,* says Robert Graves, is the oldest novel in the history of literature, though it may be that *Gilgamesh* is an older one. In either case, fantasy is there, complete with witches, battles with monsters, curses, ventures to the very brink of hell itself. Good fantasy, too, because when we read those books the happenings seem real to us."

He paused a moment. Then:

"Here as Americans, we began early. The witchcraft reports of Cotton Mather can be a good place to start. When we became our own nation, there was fantasy with Washington Irving, Edgar Allan Poe, Nathaniel Hawthorne—on ahead to Mark Twain, who spent his boyhood on a marvel-conscious frontier and who at the end of his career wrote *The Mysterious Stranger,* with a final chapter that will make your hair stand up and give you nightmares. And in the twentieth century, Scott Fitzgerald wrote fantasy, and so did William Faulkner, and so do writers today. Read the bestseller lists, and you'll find their works named there."

Somebody near Thunstone muttered about that. Pitt spoke on, mentioning distinguished authors past and present. "Dreams," he said. "Dreams, perhaps you call these things, as Mercutio does in *Romeo and Juliet,* 'Which are the children of an idle brain, begot of nothing but vain fantasy.' Yet Charles Dickens didn't disdain to dream, and wrote *A Christmas Carol.* Nor did H. G. Wells, with his strange stories, unbelievably believable. Fantastic dreams become wakeaday facts. As facts they become commonplaces, and we split the atom and fly to the moon and cure the plagues we thought were incurable. We mustn't dismiss dreams as idle, our own dreams or the dreams of others. Because dreams keep coming true."

He came to a close. "This afternoon, at three o'clock,

THE SCHOOL OF DARKNESS 133

we'll hear Professor Tashiro Shimada," he said. "Whatever he may tell us, I predict it will be interesting. And tonight after dinner, at eight o'clock, our speaker will be John Thunstone, about whose accomplishments I could talk forever. But I'm through up here now."

There was loud applause, and everyone rose and babbled together. Yet again Thunstone looked here and there for a sign of Grizel Fian or Rowley Thorne. If they were present, they contrived to be invisible.

He and Sharon went along the aisle and Reuben Manco and Father Bundren came behind them, and back of them Shimada and Kyoki and Layton.

"I'd advise that we should stay together," said Father Bundren. "Without pretending to any extrasensory perception, I feel that our enemies are growing fairly desperate, and they'll try some desperate move."

"That's true talk," approved Manco. "Where shall we go?"

"Why not to my room?" offered Thunstone. "We can have some lunch sent up, and consider whatever had better be considered."

"And Layton and I will go to my quarters," said Kyoki from behind.

He and Layton headed across the campus. The other party went to the Inn and to the elevator. Thunstone thought that they moved as a purposeful escort to Sharon, and was glad for this sturdy companionship. In his room, he gave Sharon the most comfortable chair and put Father Bundren in the other. Manco sat on the floor in a corner, his legs crossed. Thunstone and Shimada sat together on the bed. Thunstone kept his cane on the spread beside him.

"We seem to have organized ourselves as some sort of brain trust," said Father Bundren. "I hope we qualify. What first?"

"Smoke first," declared Manco, fetching out his stone ele-

134 THE SCHOOL OF DARKNESS

phant pipe. "Ritual smoke. Indians always start councils with that."

Thunstone handed him a pouch. Manco zipped it open and sniffed thoughtfully.

"This will be good," he announced. "Kinnickinnick, *yuh,* and bark of red willow in with the tobacco. Strong medicine."

"It was mixed for me by my friend Long Spear," Thunstone told him. "He's of the Tsichah tribe, and he's a chief and a medicine man, like you."

"Strong medicine," said Manco again, and carefully filled the pipe. From his pocket he brought a wooden match, snapped it afire on his thumbnail, and kindled the mixture in the bowl of the pipe. He drew a lungful of the smoke and blew it out in a blue cloud. Then he leaned to hand the pipe to Sharon.

"You too," he said. "For strength, for safety."

Sharon put the stem between her red lips, inhaled diffidently, and blew out her own cloud. She passed the pipe to Thunstone on the bed. He smoked in turn and handed the thing on to Shimada, who followed suit and gave the pipe to Father Bundren. The priest blew smoke and returned the pipe to Manco.

"Now," said Manco, "pray to your gods, all of you."

Again he emitted clouds, to the north, the west, the south, the east, and up and finally down. The six directions, Thunstone recognized, each with its own sacred significance. Sitting silently as Manco accomplished his ritual, Thunstone said a prayer deep within himself. Shimada and Father Bundren held their heads low; they must have been praying, too. And Sharon bowed and clasped her hands devoutly. Quiet hung in the room, for about ten seconds.

At last Manco laid his pipe aside and looked around at them. "We are ready now," he said, in the deep voice that Indians use for formal pronouncements.

THE SCHOOL OF DARKNESS 135

"Could we be ready for lunch, perhaps?" asked Thunstone. "What would you like?"

"I leave the ordering to you," said Shimada. "For myself, I do not feel that I require much just now."

"Nor do I," said Sharon. "Nor I," added Father Bundren. And Manco lifted a brown hand, as though in endorsement.

"I would be glad for just a sandwich," said Sharon.

Thunstone took the telephone and called room service. He ordered ham and cheese sandwiches and a pot of coffee. While they waited, they talked of what would happen, of what might possibly happen.

"When I speak this afternoon, I mean to be frank about the situation here," declared Shimada. "Maybe I won't name names, but I'll go into interesting details." He smiled. "Embarrassing details, perhaps. To bring them more into the open. You will be enchanted with what I say, I promise you. Yes, that much of a promise, at least."

"I'm always enchanted with what you say," said Father Bundren, "just as, so far, I'm not enchanted with what Rowley Thorne and Grizel Fian may say."

They looked at each other, all around the room. Thunstone spoke.

"It's up to us to come to a practical solution of what seems to be a downright unknown situation," he said. "Be a brain trust, as Father Bundren puts it. Work together as a unit, for mutual defense and offense. Find out what they'll try next, and head them back."

"They hate us," said Sharon softly.

"Hate is an active principle with them," nodded Father Bundren. "They not only hate us, they hate all humanity— they hate each other, they hate themselves. Here I'm at a disadvantage. As a priest, it's up to me to love all humanity, love every living soul. Can love be stronger than hate?"

136   THE SCHOOL OF DARKNESS

"I would say no to that," spoke up Manco from where he squatted. "Hate doesn't owe anything to anybody."

A knock at the door, and Thunstone opened it. A waiter wheeled in a cart with a great tray of sandwiches, a coffee pot and cups. Thunstone paid him and gave him a tip, and they sat down and ate and talked.

"You have the right of it," said Shimada to Thunstone. "We must come to a plan of campaign here, and carry it out."

"It's our duty," said Father Bundren. "Somebody once said, duty is the most sublime word in the language."

"Wasn't that Robert E. Lee?" asked Sharon.

"Lee was a soldier, and duty was always there to be performed," said Father Bundren.

Manco, cross-legged in his corner, bit into a sandwich and sipped coffee. "Coleridge had a different view of duty. He felt that duty was imposed on all of us from childhood, by parents and teachers. And duty, he said, is a command, and every command is in the nature of an offense. Don't stare at me like that. I sit here wearing Indian beads and braids, but I did graduate from Dartmouth. They even gave me a Phi Beta Kappa key."

"Coleridge," Thunstone repeated. "He seems to have known the supernatural on close terms. Look at the fear in 'The Ancient Mariner,' in 'Christabel,' in 'Kubla Khan,' which he never finished. Which begins as a rhapsody and ends in fear."

" 'Beware, beware,' " quoted Father Bundren. " 'Close your eyes in holy dread.' But we aren't holding a literary seminar just now. We've got to settle matters with Rowley Thorne and Grizel Fian."

"Exactly," said Manco into his coffee cup.

The telephone rang. Thunstone picked it up. "Yes?" he said.

"Mr. Thunstone," came the taut voice of Grizel Fian. "I

THE SCHOOL OF DARKNESS
137

want to talk to you. Maybe come to whatever terms you want to make."

"Where are you?"

"I'm here at the Inn, I've taken a room. Number 408, on the floor above you. Will you come up? Are you afraid to come up?"

"Not in the least," he said. "I'll come there."

Rising, he picked up his cane. "Will you excuse me for a minute or so?" he asked. "Go on with your council, I'll concur in anything you decide."

"Where are you going?" Sharon asked him. "Be careful, please be careful."

"Naturally," he said and went out. He sought the stairs and mounted a flight to the corridor above. Almost at once he saw the number 408 on a door, and knocked. Grizel Fian opened it. She wore red-brown slacks and top, with a deeply scooped neckline to show the upper rises of those breasts of which she was so manifestly proud. She gazed at him with wide-drawn eyes, with a mouth that quivered.

"Come in," she said huskily.

He entered the room, looked in all corners of it. He crossed to the bathroom door, and looked to see that it was empty. He went to the closet and looked into it, too.

"No," she said, "we're all alone here."

"Forgive me, but I had to be sure," he said, with the slightest of smiles.

She sat in a chair. He sat in another, his cane in his hand.

"Suppose," she said, "that I made a virtue of necessity and ran up the white flag?"

"That would be better than running up a black one."

She fluttered her wide, bright eyes. "You're being witty, Mr. Thunstone. Let's get down to the reason I asked you to come."

"I'm waiting," he said easily.

She made a trembling gesture, palms outward. "A white

138   THE SCHOOL OF DARKNESS

flag, I said. I asked you to come and hear me say that. I want to quit."

"I've heard someone else say that."

"You mean Exum Layton. He did quit my organization, didn't he? And is he happy about it?"

"More or less, it seems," said Thunstone.

"All right, all right. What if I were to do the same? What if I disbanded the worship I've conducted here? Gave it up? Confessed I was wrong—"

"And what might Rowley Thorne think about that?"

She tossed her head. Her hair stirred as if blown in a breeze.

"Rowley Thorne is here because I could call him here," she said. "Call him out of the strange land where he was a prisoner. I could help you dispose of him again."

"Very likely you could, if you mean what you say."

Her face clamped fiercely into deep lines. "You think I'm lying," she accused.

Thunstone's smile grew wide. "I'm afflicted to say, that's just what I think."

She was silent then, her eyes as bright and hard as jewels. At last:

"They say you're a brave man," she said between clenched teeth. "Is it brave to insult a woman?"

"I make a virtue of necessity, too," said Thunstone. "I have something to do in this town and on this campus, and I've learned to smell a trap set for me. You say that I insult you because I don't believe you, but I'd be a damned fool if I did believe you."

"All right, it's war again!" she half screamed at him.

"Now you do tell the truth," he smiled, still more widely.

She sprang from her chair, flung her arms out, and began to babble what must have been a curse, in a language Thunstone did not know. He half drew his silver blade. The hilt

THE SCHOOL OF DARKNESS　　　139

sang in his hand. Grizel Fian walked across the floor, then swung around to glare at him.

"Get out!" she spat.

He rose and bowed. "I'll be only too glad to."

He went out at the door and closed it carefully behind him. He could hear her furious voice, but could not make out the words. Back he went and down the stairs and again to his own room. The others looked up at him as he entered.

"Well, now what?" demanded Manco.

"I was talking to Grizel Fian. She said she wanted to quit her devil worship and be on our side. Help us defeat Rowley Thorne."

"From what I know of her so far, I'd say she was lying," said Sharon, speaking strongly for the first time since they had come together that morning. "She was trying to trick you."

"I felt that I had to say that very thing to her," said Thunstone. "And it made her angry. She said some kind of curse on me and told me to get out. So I got out and came back here. You see, they're still very much at war with us. War—she used that word to me."

"*Yuh,*" boomed out Manco. "War. But I come from a people good at all kinds of war. Many times, we win our wars."

"We came to a sort of decision, and we hope you'll be with us on it," Father Bundren said to Thunstone. "We stay together all the time and try to force them into the open. Then we do our own best to bring the whole matter to a close, this very night."

"Somehow," said Manco, half to himself.

"When I speak in a little while, I will make them a challenge," said Shimada. "I will name names. I will say what they have in mind as I see it. I would like to talk to young Oishi Kyoki, but he wanted to spend the morning in meditation."

140   THE SCHOOL OF DARKNESS

"Second sight?" asked Sharon.

"Second sight, if you will. He would try to see and hear at a distance."

"You'll say all those things when you speak today," said Thunstone to Shimada.

"And after me, you speak tonight," said Shimada. "You will follow up, you will close in on them. Bring them to what will be the end of this struggle."

Thunstone gazed at him for a moment, wondering how he would manage to do that. Finally he said, "All right. I'm with you. I said I'd be with you, and I meant it."

Shimada looked at the watch on his wrist. It was square and brilliantly jeweled, on a broad gold band figured in green.

"It comes to the time when I must go and say what I will say," he said. "I would be glad if all of you came to hear."

"That's exactly what we intend to do," Father Bundren assured him. "We'll follow you over to that auditorium."

XII

They walked out together, crossed the street, and headed for the auditorium. Shimada moved nimbly at the head of their group. Next came Thunstone and Sharon, her hand holding his arm confidently while his other hand carried his cane. At the rear were Father Bundren and Manco, talking as though to some good purpose. Thunstone glanced from one to another of his comrades, and to the third. These were three wise men, each strong and confident in his special conviction, the best allies he could hope for.

Inside the auditorium, again a great, jabbering throng of people. The speeches were drawing interested crowds. Lee Pitt met Shimada and they headed for the stage entrance. The others sat in a row together, Thunstone, then Sharon, then Father Bundren, then Manco. Thunstone gazed around him at the audience. Well back in it sat Grizel Fian, in her bright red dress.

"She's here," he reported, "but not Rowley Thorne."

"Who can tell that?" asked Manco from beyond Father Bundren. "Maybe he's here. Maybe he can be unseen."

"I somehow think I'd know," said Thunstone.

Up on the stage, Pitt was introducing Shimada. Shimada came to the lectern. His teeth and his spectacles shone. He made a slight, swift bow.

"How gratifying to me that so many have come to hear what I may say," he began. "Gratifying and flattering. I can't truly promise that all of you will like what I am going

142 THE SCHOOL OF DARKNESS

to tell you, but I think that all of you will find things of interest in it."

Again a bow.

"In Japan these days, especially in our cities, you might feel that we Japanese are like you Westerners," he went on. "Especially our young people, our modern opposite numbers of your students here at Buford State University. Those young people over there like to wear jeans and T-shirts with figures and slogans. They listen to rock and roll music, and they rock and roll with it. They play video games, play them well. They eat hamburgers and hot dogs—lots of those. Eat them gladly. In Japan, we busily manufacture computers and automobiles and sell them here in America. Yes, and television sets—I would conjecture that, among you who have television, your sets are made in Japan for the most part. Here and there in our cities, you might feel that you were in San Francisco or Chicago."

Again a pause, a study of the audience.

"Yes," said Shimada, "we Japanese are good at learning new things, new truths. We prosper in industry and commerce as we do in arts. But we do not forget the old truths, we do not leave them behind."

Now Shimada was in dead earnest. His spectacled eyes roamed here and there over the listeners.

"I promised you that I would say something about Japanese beliefs, I promised you that when I spoke briefly at the first session of this meeting. Mankind is very old on this planet, was struggling hard to be mankind millions of years ago. In Japan, mankind was present and doing quite well indeed, about two hundred thousand years back, or earlier. Those first Japanese could make fire, had fine flint tools, had community life, and must have had a sense of the unseen world that was, though unseen, manifest. Somewhere far back—before written language, before surviving reports—

THE SCHOOL OF DARKNESS 143

the Japanese had a special religion of their own. What is called Shinto today."

He gazed around the auditorium again. "Do some of you know about Shinto?" he asked.

Here and there, hands went up. Not many.

"Then some of you have information," said Shimada. "Let me speak briefly and simply to the others, something about Shinto. For one thing, as I have said, it is so old a religious philosophy that there can be no tracing of its beginnings. There are books of guidance—the *Kojiki* and the *Nihongi*—but those were recent, written no longer ago than the eighth century. Buddhism came to Japan as a comparatively new faith and grew strong, yet Shinto remained the official state religion until it was formally disestablished on December 15, 1945, at the end of that tragic war. Our emperor Hirohito renounced his traditional claim to descent from the sun goddess Amaterasu. But Shinto has survived. It helps its believers. It helps them here in Buford."

Again he let his words sink in.

"For, yes, we have Shinto here in Buford," he went on. "Shinto, that was born in Japan, and was greatly significant in Japan before Buddhism came, hat in hand, to ask admittance. Shinto—*Kaminomioomichi,* it is described. *Kami* is sometimes translated in the West as the name of God. It may be better translated as power of good against evil, right against wrong, if we can be wise enough to tell the difference between right and wrong."

He spread his slim, tea-colored hands, as though in appeal. "I am well aware that I am no true authority on Shinto. I am not a holy man, only an educator, to some extent a scholar and an educator. You have had holy men on this platform before me. Reuben Manco is a medicine man of his impressive Cherokee faith. Father Mark Bundren is a Catholic priest, of the scholarly Jesuitical order. I say again that my Shintoism is nowhere complete, but there

144 THE SCHOOL OF DARKNESS

is a scholar here in Buford, profound in its teachings and a partaker in its powers, whose help is great. Never mind his name. As things are here, he's better unknown than known."

All these things Shimada had said with the utmost calm and clarity, as though he were lecturing a class. But the whole audience listened attentively. Thunstone spared a glance toward where Grizel Fian sat. She leaned forward in her seat, raptly intent on what Shimada had said. He went on:

"Here, then, is the fundamental belief of Shinto, and it proves the ancient basis of Shinto: There is life in all things, and not only life, but sense, awareness. I know the fashionable arguments that plants live and feel, and why did we need to be told that? We see that trees and flowers and grasses are living things. There are those who say that we should talk to plants—but Shintoists have talked to plants for many thousands of years. And not only to plants, but to stones, rivers, ponds, houses, all things. Shinto says that this auditorium has life and sense, not only the whole structure but each separate stone and brick in it. If one is strong enough, schooled enough, in Shinto, he can speak to this whole world and every living thing in it—whether animal, vegetable or mineral—and hear every living thing as it replies."

Again he gestured his appeal. "Is that not good to have, such a voice to speak to all things and such an ear to hear the answers? I say that it can be achieved, that it is here in your city and on your campus, and you can believe or disbelieve. I say that this ear, this voice, operate here, and just now, in the service of Shinto which is good, it reveals things which are evil."

A murmur at that. Thunstone, glancing around, saw the huge, bearded man who had played Hume at the Playmakers Theater, had been at the ceremony in Grizel

THE SCHOOL OF DARKNESS 145

Fian's basement, had pursued him in the cemetery. He leaned powerfully forward, his heavy muscles bunching inside his denim jacket. He seemed almost ready to rise, to say something. Shimada saw his motion, recognized him, and smiled as though in recognition.

"I want to tell some diverting stories," he said. He told the stories. They dealt with various men and women, whose Japanese names were hard to understand, and their supernatural difficulties. Into one story came a malignant fox, into another a friendly badger. Evil forces lurked in the stories, and were detected and defeated by experts in Shinto.

"You think these things are fables?" asked Shimada. "I venture to assure you of the contrary. They are matter-of-fact records, well authenticated and known to students. But what is all this to the point, ladies and gentlemen? My duty is to speak of conditions here and now. Here and now in Buford. The apostles of hate and destruction are here among us. Shinto reveals them. Shall I name names? Then suppose I begin with a name well known in this community, the name of—"

He paused. Then: "The name of Grizel Fian!" he fairly shouted into the microphone.

A stir, a bustle among the listeners. "No!" cried someone.

"Yes," insisted Shimada, more quietly but forcefully for all that. "Grizel Fian, whose selections from Shakespeare we witnessed on the campus last night. Who leads a following of deluded disciples to do whatever perverted evil comes into their heads. Who means to use this university to promote her gospel of anarchic evil."

"That's a lie!" roared out the big man.

"A truth," came back Shimada. "John Keats once said that beauty is truth, truth beauty. But truth can be ugly things, and I am telling you one of them. I am afflicted to have to accuse a woman, but with Grizel Fian this is necessary. She represents a night side of infamies that has af-

146   THE SCHOOL OF DARKNESS

flicted you since this school's beginning, and I mean to make my charge clear."

Somebody sprang up in a section of the audience away from where Thunstone and the others sat. It was red-clad Grizel Fian. Her dress fluttered as she fairly ran up the aisle and toward the door and out. She was like a scarlet bird in flight.

"Sayonara," called Shimada after her. "Goodbye."

The giant man was up and out of his seat and into the aisle. He loomed there. "Look here, you," he blustered at the top of his voice. "You're no gentleman to talk like that to Grizel. You'll be sorry about this."

"I am already sorry that I had to speak to her so," Shimada said back. "But you Occidentals have a proverb— Needs must when the Devil drives—and the Devil is out here in Buford, whip in hand."

"I'll make you shut up!"

"Will you indeed?" Shimada said silkily. "How will you go about that? Would you like to come up on the platform with me, or shall I come down there to you? Remember how you tried it last night, and how it turned out. These people might be amused to watch you and me fight for, say, thirty seconds. It should not take me longer than that."

"My name is—"

"I don't care to hear your name," said Shimada.

The big man turned and fled up the aisle, as hurriedly as had Grizel Fian. Shimada watched him go, took off his spectacles and wiped them carefully on his handkerchief, and put them on again. He returned to the microphone.

"My apologies," he said, his voice gentler than ever. "My apologies for this interruption. I am deeply hurt that those two wanted to leave, but the rest of you are still here. Unless others want to go also, want to be where they will not hear the rest of what I have come to say to you."

THE SCHOOL OF DARKNESS

147

There was a stir in the audience, but nobody else got up and went away.

"Then let me continue," said Shimada. "Let me go on with what some of us have been at pains to find out here." He bowed briefly above the microphone. "About the evil that has been here, grown here, since the founding of this school."

They listened. All of them listened.

"In the beginning, devils were worshiped here. When Buford got money to found its college those long years ago, there was also money to prosper the cult of evil, prosper it to this day. Grizel Fian has been its latest leader, its queen. She has had a considerable ally by the name of Rowley Thorne. Do you know that name?"

He waited. Everyone sat still. Nobody spoke or gestured.

"I am certain that some of you do know Rowley Thorne. If so, you know he has suffered defeat here. He suffered it twice last night. I have witnessed those defeats. Rowley Thorne, ladies and gentlemen, is a renowned sorcerer and evildoer, but just now he is a loser. And we who have defeated him are winners and are strengthened by winning. He and his companions are weakened by losing."

They sat and listened. Thunstone could see the red-haired girl he knew. Perhaps she was staying to make report to her comrades.

"Reduced to its simplest terms, the conflict is understandable," said Shimada. "It is between good and evil, if you know what is good and what is evil. Decide on that for yourselves."

He walked clear away from the lectern and the microphone. He held out his hands.

"It is between love and hate!" he cried, so loudly, that his unamplified voice rang through the auditorium. "Which of those will win? Wait until tonight. I think all this will be decided. Decided definitely."

148   THE SCHOOL OF DARKNESS

He bowed low. He raised his hands before him. Still bowing low, he moved backward, across the stage, into the wings and out of sight.

And silence. It was an oppressive silence. Nobody applauded. Nobody moved.

Lee Pitt appeared and came to the microphone.

"Tonight, at eight o'clock, we will hear from John Thunstone," he said, and no more.

People rose, moved along the aisles. They chattered, as usual, but it was subdued chatter. Thunstone and Sharon and their companions walked out in a group. Shimada came to join them. The light and the air outside were like a release.

Someone confronted them on the sidewalk in front. It was the red-haired girl who had been at the theater, who had been at the witch ceremony in Grizel Fian's basement. Her hair was disordered, her face was pale. Makeup stood out on it, grotesque patches of makeup.

"Did you have to do what you did?" she burst out at Shimada. "Did you have to say those things about Grizel?"

"Indeed, I felt that I had to," said Shimada courteously. "Did I not tell the truth?"

"You'll pay for this!"

"I shall pay whatever is honestly due, whenever you present your bill."

She shifted her angry gaze to Sharon. "And as for you—"

"Won't you please go?" Thunstone interrupted.

The girl turned and hurried off across the campus. They watched her go, then went on, crossed to the Inn, and entered the lobby. They found a group of chairs and a sofa, where they all sat down together.

"*Ahi,*" intoned Manco. "I'd say it's working, that they're coming out into the open, to be seen and faced."

"And they do not know what to do," added Shimada.

THE SCHOOL OF DARKNESS

"They are afraid. Maybe fear will help them. It's supposed to stimulate the thyroid, suprarenal and pituitary glands."

"But do we know what to do?" asked Thunstone, and all of them looked at him fixedly.

"We'll cue ourselves by what you yourself do," said Father Bundren. "When you speak tonight. That will be after dark, and I judge that they'll have to make their decisive move, then and there. What are you going to say to the people, to back up what Professor Shimada began?"

Thunstone shook his massive head. "I had some notes, but as of just now they're no good anymore. I'm afraid I'll be up there ad-libbing, playing it by ear."

"*Ahi,* good," said Manco. "Your words will be strong, the words of a chief."

"I hope so," said Thunstone. "It strikes me that I'm the one who has talked with these devil people more than any of you. They've tried to frighten me, they've tried to cajole me. But their talk is empty. Banal."

"Clichés," supplied Father Bundren. "Is that it?"

"That's it exactly," said Thunstone. "They say things out of their teachings, words that have been chewed over already. They're like people mouthing crazy religious or political jargon. It's—well, it's colorless. I can't think of any other word for it."

"But what you are going to say will force these devil followers," said Manco. "And we others, we will be there with you, to back you up."

"Yes," said Shimada. "I say, it is for us all to be on stage but out of sight in the wings, ready."

"Good," said Manco again, and, "Good," Father Bundren echoed him.

Shimada was frowning slightly. "I could wish for my young friend Oishi," he said. "He can see and hear into these matters so much better than I do. I wish he were here."

150 THE SCHOOL OF DARKNESS

"Your wish comes true," said Manco, looking toward the outer door. "Here he comes, just as you say his name."

They all looked. Oishi Kyoki ran across the floor toward them. Shimada rose to meet him. Kyoki spoke, a rattling flood of Japanese. Shimada stared.

"He tells us that Exum Layton, poor Exum Layton, has died suddenly," Shimada said.

XIII

They were all on their feet at once, even Sharon. Kyoki stood among them, trembling. His eyes stared. His face that had been brown looked gray, bloodless.

"Tell us how it happened," Shimada said to him. "Speak English."

"It just happened," said Kyoki. "We had been together at my room. I was sensing some unusual things. He seemed to be all right then. Perhaps I did not pay attention, I was deep in seeing, in hearing. I had tried to see and hear Rowley Thorne—I had a sense of blood, a blood sacrifice—"

"How did this poor man die?" broke in Shimada.

"We looked at our watches. We thought that you had nearly finished speaking, and we left to come to you here, at the Inn. We walked together on the campus. We talked. Poor Exum, he seemed all right then. But as we came to the center of the campus, he made a moaning noise— *Mmmmmm!* And down he fell."

"Dead?"

"Dead at once, I think. He fell and he lay. I knelt to touch him—he did not breathe. Others came to see, a call was made for the campus police. They got an ambulance, took him to the hospital. The ambulance men said that he had died."

"How?" said Sharon. "How did he die?"

"Rowley Thorne and Grizel Fian can kill at a distance," said Thunstone. "Say certain words, point a certain way. They tried it on me last night, but it didn't work."

152   THE SCHOOL OF DARKNESS

Father Bundren bowed his head.

"Exum Layton died in the hands of God," he said. "I'd heard his confession, I had told him that his sins were forgiven. He had repented."

"You say they took him to the hospital," said Thunstone. "We'd better go there. Where is it—the hospital?"

"Not far." Kyoki pointed somewhere. "Edge of the campus. Half a mile, maybe."

"Then let's go," said Thunstone. "You too, Sharon. Don't ever get out of my sight."

"I have protection," she half whispered. "My cross and the bell you gave me."

But she came. They went out and across the campus, Kyoki leading the way. They came to the University library, walked down steps beside it, crossed another street and a big parking lot. At the far side they mounted another flight of stairs, made of iron like a fire escape, and came out upon the hospital grounds. Kyoki still led the way swiftly. Sharon had almost to trot to keep up. He brought them to a pillared entrance where cars stopped and started again, where people came in and out, some in wheelchairs. Inside the lobby was a long desk with businesslike young women sitting in a row behind. One of these heard their errand, frowned hesitatingly over it, then made a telephone call. They waited, and a plump man came into view and joined them.

"I'm Dr. Harold Forrester," he introduced himself. "A pathologist. What's the problem here, and how can I help you?"

Thunstone explained their wish for information as to Layton's death. Dr. Forrester listened, nodding importantly.

"Mr. Layton was pronounced dead on arrival," he said. "No marks of violence on him. It seems to have been a sudden stoppage of the heart action, but we can't be sure. We're trying to locate any relatives or close friends."

THE SCHOOL OF DARKNESS 153

"He had no relatives," said Thunstone, "and I'd judge that we were his only true friends when he died. Lately he had severed relations with a group of others. We'd like to speak for arrangements."

Dr. Forrester squinted at him. "You're quite sure about no relatives? Dr. Lee Pitt was his faculty adviser, and he says about the same thing."

"When it comes to that, I was his spiritual advisor," said Father Bundren. "He told me that he had no relatives, none at all."

"Do you want to see him?" asked Forrester. "Come along with me."

He led them to a flight of stairs going down. Below were bleak halls, with doors to laboratories and storage rooms. Forrester opened a metal door and ushered them into a long slice of a chamber with pallid fluorescent lights. Its ceiling and one side wall were of blue-gray tile. The other side showed hatchlike doors of stainless steel. There was a closeness in the air, a hush. Forrester checked along the doors and opened one. He drew out a sort of great tray with a silent body upon it.

Instantly Thunstone recognized Exum Layton, covered to his naked chest with a sheet. His face was blank and dully pale. His eyes were closed. His mustache straggled.

"There's no mark on him, no indication of any injury," Dr. Forrester told them again. "No external evidence of anything like poison of any kind. I feel that we'd like permission for somebody to do an autopsy."

"Since he hasn't any family, can't we speak as his friends?" asked Thunstone. "Say that we're in favor of an autopsy?"

Dr. Forrester pondered that. "Let me have you talk to our director," he said. "He's Dr. Clark, Dr. Christopher Clark."

They went upstairs into the lobby again. Dr. Forrester

154 THE SCHOOL OF DARKNESS

took a telephone at the desk and talked earnestly into it. Then, "Come with me," he said, and they went by elevator to an upper floor. In a front office there, a secretary bade them, "Please go in," and Forrester ushered them into the room behind. It was an imposing place, with file cabinets against most of the walls and a single oil painting of a landscape that seemed to be English countryside. At a paper-stacked desk sat a blocky man in a beautifully cut blazer of dark blue. He wore a gray beard, also beautifully cut and carefully brushed. Rising, he responded to Forrester's introductions.

"I know who you are, Mr. Thunstone," he said. "I've read about you in various journals. Are those accounts true?"

"Not always," said Thunstone.

"I promise myself great profit in hearing you speak tonight." Dr. Clark studied Manco, who stood with brown expressionless face between the brackets of his braids. "Chief," he said, "I could wish you'd lecture our pre-meds, on Indian medicines."

"Wagh," Manco said in his deep voice of formality. "They'd not believe."

"But sit down, sit down," said Dr. Clark. "We have chairs enough here. Let's go into this problem about the body of—what was his name?"

"Exum Layton," said Sharon.

"Yes, yes. What an unfortunate matter. Mr. Thunstone, you and your friends ask to speak and decide as his close friends. Of course there will be some expenses, here and also for some sort of funeral."

"I'll stand good for those expenses," said Thunstone promptly. "I happen to be solvent. I can give you the address of my bank in New York and of my investment broker."

THE SCHOOL OF DARKNESS   155

"And I'll conduct the funeral service," added Father Bundren. "I'll stay over in Buford to do that."

"You're kind," said Dr. Clark. "Gracious. Just what I'd expect."

He took up a telephone and talked to the secretary in the front office. She brought in papers, which all of them signed. Then they gave their addresses at the Inn, and left. The air outside seemed bright, but away somewhere sounded a mutter as of distant thunder.

"Thunder on the left," said Thunstone, walking along with Sharon. "That's supposed to be a warning of some important happening to come."

"We don't need thunder to tell us that," said Manco. As he walked, he filled his pipe from the pouch that held his ritually mixed tobacco and herbs. He popped a wooden match alight on his thumbnail, lighted the pipe and puffed, then handed it to Thunstone.

"Smoke," he said. "All of you smoke. Pray while you smoke."

Thunstone drew a mouthful of the pungent vapor and passed the pipe to Sharon. She also puffed and held the pipe behind her to Shimada, who was talking earnestly in Japanese to Kyoki. They drew smoke, and then Father Bundren. The pipe came back to Manco, who tapped it clean and stowed it away.

"*Ahi,*" he said. "Professor Shimada, you spoke today about attempted murder. I call this an attempted murder that succeeded."

"How did they manage it?" asked Sharon.

"It's done everywhere," said Manco. "My friend Thunstone says they tried to manage it with him last night. I've studied reports. People are prayed to death in a hundred ways. It happens in the South Seas, in Italy, in New York. Among Indian tribes. Everywhere."

Sharon's blue eyes were daunted. "Poor Exum Layton,"

156 THE SCHOOL OF DARKNESS

she said to Thunstone. "He looked so small, somehow, lying there."

"The dead always seem to shrink," Thunstone told her, remembering experiences of his own.

"Their souls depart," said Father Bundren from behind. "I predict that the autopsy will indicate that his heart just stopped. And it did stop—it was stopped with a murderous vengeance. High time that those who stopped it were stopped from doing more evils." He drew a deep breath. "But he died a believer. He was killed for being a believer. His soul has rest."

"Yes, it does," said Sharon. Then again to Thunstone, hand on his arm: "You said you'd assume those expenses for him. That will run into money."

"Nothing I can't afford," he said.

"Listen. Let me share the expenses with you."

"But—"

"Yes, let her," put in Manco. "She wants to help. Her help makes her one of us, more than ever. She says a good thing."

"Well," said Thunstone, "all right, Sharon."

She smiled up at him and her hand squeezed his arm tightly.

Shimada and Kyoki kept on talking in Japanese. At last Shimada looked at his watch.

"It is just past five o'clock," he reported in English. "Oishi here has some suggestions for what to do."

"Let's all go to my room," invited Thunstone. "Maybe have a drink there. We'll talk for a while and then go to dinner together."

"Dinner?" repeated Sharon. "Do you think of dinner?"

"I'm thinking of it now," replied Thunstone. "I want to eat well before I speak, before whatever happens when I speak."

THE SCHOOL OF DARKNESS 157

"Something will happen," vowed Manco. "Or will try to happen."

"Something we won't let happen," said Father Bundren stoutly. "We've defeated them again and again, except in the case of poor Exum Layton. Whatever they try to do, we won't let it happen."

"No," said Kyoki. "No."

They reached the Inn, went up to Thunstone's room. Kyoki went out to bring back a supply of ice. Thunstone brought another bottle of brandy out of his suitcase and found glasses for all. They sat wherever they could. Sharon was in the armchair, Shimada on the straight one. Thunstone and Father Bundren sat together on the bed. Both Manco and Kyoki were on the floor, cross-legged. All sipped the brandy thoughtfully.

"Mr. Thunstone," said Shimada at last, "we are your guests here, and all of us, I think, feel that you are the special target chosen by the enemy. Let us call you the chairman of this committee. Speak first."

"If that's the will of all of you, let me start by summing up what we've summed up before," said Thunstone. "These creatures—Rowley Thorne and Grizel Fian and their followers—have been defeated several times. They grew desperate, and they killed Exum Layton. I agree with the thought that when I speak tonight they'll try to do something to strike me permanently silent. Some other spell, perhaps, to kill me as they killed Layton."

"*Wagh,*" boomed Manco. "I've said that there are many ways to kill. The bad spirits of the Cherokee know those ways. It is for a medicine man to defend against them."

"Sir," said Kyoki beside him. "Chief, should I call you? You speak again and again like somebody who instinctively understands Shinto. How did you learn?"

"I learned young," said Manco. "When I was a boy, I was taken to raise by an old medicine man. Tsukala was his

158 THE SCHOOL OF DARKNESS

name. He taught me to get up early and sing the sunrise song. He taught me to listen, as he told tales of the world's early times, when men and animals and plants all lived and talked together as friends and neighbors."

"That is true Shinto teaching," offered Shimada, and, "Yes," said Kyoki.

"Tsukala taught me the use of plants for medicine, for charms, for protection," Manco went on. "He taught me the secret songs and prayers. He built a sacred fire, and told me to tend it for long days and long nights. He put sacred herbs into the fire, and I breathed their vapors. When I dreamed, he told me how to read what the dreams meant. Under his guidance, I performed many things. Sometimes frightening things. When Tsukala died, the people called me their medicine man. I have been a medicine man ever since. I am one now. This buckskin shirt I wear is a medicine man's shirt, the beads on it make strong magic. My work is to find out dangers and drive them back, to cure sickness, to gather wisdom where I can and use it to help others."

"Shinto," said Kyoki to him. "That is Shinto you describe."

"*Wagh,*" said Manco. "It is the belief of my people." He looked around at the others. "There are several beliefs here, several roads. All roads are good if they bring us to good things."

"Yes, that is Shinto you speak," declared Shimada. "You American Indians have been here a long time, tens of thousands of years. Yet, before you came from Asia, Shinto was a developing fact in Japan. Perhaps your people brought some Shinto teachings along, and keep them to this day."

"*Wagh,*" said Manco again. He was smoking his elephant pipe. "There's much in what you say, but we're here to make a plan for tonight, when Thunstone speaks."

Kyoki seemed to stare into space. "They plan, too. Plan against us. They are careful, they try to think behind a wall.

THE SCHOOL OF DARKNESS 159

But I know this much, they plan murderously." He looked at Thunstone. "Plan murderously against you. I see their thoughts, your image in their thoughts. And there is blood on your image."

"What will you do?" Father Bundren asked Thunstone.

"Do? I'll get up there and tell them to their faces. Dare them."

"We'd all better be up on stage with you," said Father Bundren. "Out of sight of the audience, but up there. Ready to make a stand in force, so to speak."

"What do you expect to happen, Father?" asked Sharon.

"My child, I don't know what to expect. Maybe to expect everything."

"Suspect everything," said Manco, puffing smoke. "Be ready to fight it."

"Let me be there," said Sharon.

"Of course," said Thunstone. "You must be with us at all times. And you must carry protection, all the time."

"This." She touched the cross at her neck. "And this." She held out the silver bell. It whispered its music.

"I'll be protected, too," declared Thunstone. "My cane and its silver blade. And wait, something else."

He reached to the bureau for the book that lay there. "The *Long Lost Friend,*" he said. "John George Hohman's talisman against spiritual dangers. Father Bundren, you questioned this once, then you seemed to endorse it."

"It worked well for us," said the priest. He took the book and opened to its preface.

" 'Whoever carries this book with him is safe from all his enemies, visible or invisible,' " he read aloud. "I pray that this will be true for you."

"I pray the same," said Sharon.

"It says that you can't die without the 'holy corpse' of Jesus Christ," said Father Bundren, still studying the pref-

160   THE SCHOOL OF DARKNESS

ace. "Let me say that, when all things are settled, I'll administer the sacrament to you. Not until then."

Shimada took the book in turn and leafed through it. "Many good things are in here," he said, and passed it back to Thunstone, who slid it into the side pocket of his jacket.

"It is well for you to have that strong protection," said Shimada. "For Oishi and me, there is Shinto. We are grateful for Shinto."

"I have my strong medicine shirt, and I have this," said Manco, displaying his elephant pipe. "With it goes the special tobacco."

"And I'm never without help and protection," said Father Bundren.

Thunstone rose from where he sat and picked up his sword cane.

"I'd say that we're all as ready as possible," he said. "Let's go and have some dinner."

They went out together. It seemed to Thunstone that they walked purposefully along the corridor to the elevator. They were, he thought again, like a fighting force, ready to meet any threat. Even Sharon was ready.

XIV

Entering the dining room, they found a table where all six of them could sit. A waiter came quickly to hand menus around. Thunstone had not noticed this waiter before. He was a slim young man, with dark hair carefully combed to his head, and his white jacket seemed to have been tailored to him.

Sharon ordered a lamb chop and some green vegetables. Shimada and Kyoki asked for servings of something made with shrimps and rice. Thunstone brooded over the menu.

"I see I can get a small sirloin steak," he said. "Let me have it rare, and a baked potato and a salad." He smiled around at his companions. "That's more or less the pregame meal we used to have back when I played football."

"You make a wise choice," said Father Bundren. "I think I'll have the same."

"And so shall I," said Manco. "And black coffee."

They all ordered coffee and the young waiter went away to the kitchen. Thunstone narrowed his eyes and thought. He was to speak. He must speak. He wouldn't use the speech he had prepared. Shimada had begun for him. He would finish.

"A pregame meal," Father Bundren was saying. "When I was younger, I played football, too. I had those pregame meals. Those were balanced. The steak was protein, and the baked potato was for carbohydrate."

"We'd eat well before game time, about ten o'clock in the

162 THE SCHOOL OF DARKNESS

morning," said Thunstone. "And no butter on the potato in those far-off days, but I'm going to have some now."

"The meat is for strength," intoned Manco. "Man is himself a creature of meat. I believe in meat. I don't hold with the vegetarians."

"Leave the vegetarians alone," said Sharon. "They may not know what they're doing, but they think they do. To eat meat is to be guilty of the death of a fellow creature. Didn't Shelley say something like that?"

"And Byron liked Shelley, but he didn't agree with him there," said Father Bundren. "Neither do I."

"Thoreau," said Sharon, and Thunstone laughed.

"Thoreau was an Orientalist, he talked about being a vegetarian," he said. "But he'd catch fish and eat them—fish suffer when they're caught—and when he visited Emerson or Hawthorne, he seems to have done pretty well at eating beef or pork or whatever was on the table."

"We will face enemies who eat the flesh of killed animals," offered Shimada. "Enemies who come out of underground dens, with underground motives. From their caves, their fast places. Coming into the sun and the air, to do their enchantments. From far below."

" 'Caverns measureless to sun,' " quoted Thunstone.

"Now we're back to Coleridge," said Father Bundren. " 'Caverns measureless to man, down to a sunless sea.' But it's my notion that dark underground life isn't healthy. The sun and the air, you said, Professor Shimada. I don't believe that life is very good without sun and air. I've never tried it myself."

"Should we have wine with our dinner?" asked Shimada.

"Not for me," said Thunstone. "I'll stick to coffee with my training meal. Maybe later."

"Later," said Sharon dismally, and Thunstone shook his head at her.

"You have better faith in me than that," he chided her.

THE SCHOOL OF DARKNESS

"You've seen me deep into whatever dangers anyone dreamed up for me, and you've seen me out again."

"As you got out of your caverns," she said, not comforted. "I know that story about you over in England, and it was a miracle that you escaped there."

"It is a miracle that we have all escaped here," said Shimada. "To escape, to live, it is all a miracle."

They mused on that. The waiter brought them their coffee, and they sipped. Then he was back with a huge tray and set down their various dinners.

"Let me just say a grace," requested Father Bundren, and bowed his head. He spoke softly in Latin, then he looked up.

"I prayed for other things when I said thanks for what we're about to eat."

"About to eat," Thunstone said after him, looking at his plate.

Upon it was a steak, brown with red juices upon it, and a potato gashed open, with a big pat of butter beside it. But also on the plate lay a small heap of what looked like rosy-dark preserved fruits.

"What are those?" he asked. "You people heard me order. I didn't order those."

Shimada craned his neck to see. He studied carefully. At last he drew back and stroked his mustache.

"In Japan, they tell of certain fruits which, if you eat them with a protein, will kill you," he said. "Myself, I have never seen such things, I have never known why they do believe in them. Yet they may be in this world. They may be here as well as in Japan."

Manco struck a brown fist on the table. "Where's that waiter?" he growled. "Call him over to take them away."

"No," said Thunstone. "Leave him out of it just now."

He took a spoon and carefully scooped the fruits away

164 THE SCHOOL OF DARKNESS

into an ash tray. With a fork he pulled his steak and potato across the plate to where no fruit juice had reached.

"Maybe that was to do something to me," he said. "Maybe. If it was, the rest of my dinner should be all right."

"*Deo volente,*" said Father Bundren.

Thunstone cut the potato open more widely and put butter on its mealy interior and sprinkled salt and pepper. All watched as he trickled Worcestershire sauce on the steak and cut off a morsel and put it in his mouth. "Excellent," he announced, and took a forkful of potato to follow.

"Wait," said Father Bundren abruptly. "Don't eat any more until we share something here."

He had produced from a pocket a sort of cup. It was perhaps an inch high, and about four inches in diameter. Thunstone thought it was made of some sort of cream-tinted ivory. Its sides bore curved lines, as of a spiral. Father Bundren poured coffee from his cup into it.

"Let's all have a sip or so of this," he said, handing it to Sharon. "I've been told that to drink from that cup will ward off poisons and other assaults."

Sharon took a small mouthful. "It has a hint of perfume," she said, handing it to Shimada.

"It's supposed to be made from the horn of a unicorn," said Father Bundren.

"Really?" said Manco, taking the cup in turn. "Not of a narwhal?"

"It was given to me by an Italian priest," Father Bundren said. "It came to him from a lady who said her family had owned it for hundreds of years. She said it was from a unicorn's horn, and had great powers of protection. I can't speak positively of that, I've never brought it out to drink from until this moment, but I like to carry it with me."

The cup came to Thunstone. The coffee did have a slight taste of perfume, as Sharon had said.

"I can't speak with assurance about unicorns, either," he

THE SCHOOL OF DARKNESS

said, returning the cup to Father Bundren. "Aristotle and Pliny the Elder believed in them. So did Julius Caesar, who said they existed in Germany."

Father Bundren drank the last drops in the cup and stowed it away again. "Unicorns are mentioned in the Bible. And they were reported by early explorers in America, including missionary priests. Now then, I won't admit to beliefs about them. But in a case like ours, we shouldn't overlook a bet, anywhere along the way."

"Amen," said Manco, cutting into his steak.

The others began to eat, too. Shimada and Kyoki exclaimed over their shrimps and rice. Father Bundren and Manco ate their steaks and potatoes. Sharon toyed with her lamb chop for a while, then ate as though with a growing appetite. Thunstone carefully mixed his lettuce salad with oil and vinegar and salt and pepper. For a while, nobody talked except about the food. The Inn was a good place to eat, they agreed.

When Thunstone had finished with his steak, he beckoned the waiter. "Bring me a cup custard," he ordered.

"Let me have lime ice cream," said Sharon.

"Cup custard for me, too," said Father Bundren. "That goes with the training meal, doesn't it?"

Manco, too, ordered custard. Shimada and Kyoki did not ask for dessert. At last all had finished. Thunstone and Manco and Father Bundren produced pipes and Manco passed his pouch of mixed tobacco and herbs. Shimada kindled a cigarette. Sharon and Kyoki did not smoke.

"Whatever we make ready for, we're as ready as can be," said Manco, from within a gray cloud.

"Saint Paul spoke of being armed against evil," said Father Bundren. "He mentioned the breastplate of righteousness, the shield of salvation, the sword of the spirit. I do my best to feel righteous whenever I quote that."

166 THE SCHOOL OF DARKNESS

"Armed against evil," repeated Shimada. He brought out an envelope.

"I intended some presents to you, my friends," he said, "and it seems a good time to give them now."

He opened the envelope and spilled a red glitter of objects out on the table cloth. He picked up one. It was a bright, rubylike jewel on a length of white cord. He bowed as he handed it to Thunstone.

"Ancient Japanese charm," he said. "The red light makes the dark threat of hidden evil retire before its brightness."

He passed out other jewels on cords to Sharon, to Manco, to Father Bundren. Sharon hung hers around her neck, along with the gold cross. Manco studied his with deep-creased eyes before he tucked it away somewhere inside his beaded shirt. Father Bundren put his jewel into a pocket of his coat, and Thunstone slid his into the side pocket that held the *Long Lost Friend.* "Thank you," he said to Shimada. "I believe like you, in the power of the jewel."

"Oishi and I have them also and wear them," said Shimada. "Belief, you say. We must believe in our defenses. If we do not believe, they are not defenses."

"Without defenses, I'll be dead," said Thunstone.

"Yes," said Shimada, with a little bow. "You and all of us, for we will all be together. Live or die, we will all be together." He blinked behind his spectacles. "Or is my English not good? Should I say, we shall all be together?"

"Together, anyway," endorsed Manco. "And live. And win."

Thunstone looked at his watch. "It's past seven a good way," he said. "Maybe we ought to think about getting over there, moving in close to our work."

Their waiter passed by and Thunstone signaled for him to bring the check.

"Unusual-looking young man, that one," said Father Bundren, following the waiter with his eye. "Might he have

THE SCHOOL OF DARKNESS

been somebody in Grizel Fian's string of Shakespearean scenes?"

"If he was, I don't recognize him," said Thunstone.

The waiter came back with the bill. Thunstone signed it and laid some paper money on it. "Three dollars there for you," he said.

The waiter studied him with shadowed eyes. He picked up one of the dollars.

"Let me ask a favor of you, Mr. Thunstone," he said. "I know about you, I feel it's a privilege to talk to you. Will you autograph this dollar for me to keep, to remember you by?"

"No!" Manco almost barked, and all looked at him.

"Tell me why you brought my friend this fruit he didn't order," Manco said, pointing at it in the ash tray.

The waiter stared. "No, he didn't order that. Somebody must have put it on the plate in the kitchen."

"Who did that?" persisted Manco.

"There was a girl helping out there. Red-haired girl."

"Be easy on him, Chief," Thunstone said to Manco, and smiled up at the waiter.

"I won't sign my name for you now," he said, "but do you serve here regularly?"

"Lunch and dinner, sir."

"All right, I'll be back," Thunstone assured him. "All of us will be back, and then I'll sign just about anything. Why?"

"Oh—just—"

The waiter did not finish. He went away furtively, almost at a trot. Manco and Shimada watched him go, with narrowed eyes.

"Is he one of them?" asked Manco. "Did he want your name for something to use against you?"

"I didn't sign my name, so we can't tell," said Thunstone. They all rose. Thunstone looked toward the entrance to

168 THE SCHOOL OF DARKNESS

the lobby. For a moment, just a moment, he saw a black-clad, stocky figure there. Then it ducked out of sight, almost like a conjuring trick. As it went, he caught a glimpse of a bald head.

Sharon saw, too. "Rowley Thorne," she whispered.

"At least he didn't wait to face us," said Thunstone, and they walked into the lobby. Thorne was not there, but Lee Pitt was. He came to join them. He wore a brown raincoat and a waterproof hat.

"A storm's coming up outside," he said, "and you'd better get some foul weather gear to go out in. If you are going out."

"Naturally I'm going out," said Thunstone. "I'm going out to make some fairly bold talk."

"Well, I had a strange telephone call," said Pitt. "A woman, I don't know who, told me to advise you against appearing tonight. She said you'd try to spoil a great step forward for Buford State University."

"Ah," said Father Bundren, "might she have been Grizel Fian?"

"I said, I don't know who she was. But she was emphatic."

"Anonymous phone calls won't stop me," said Thunstone, "but I'm going to get my own raincoat."

He and Sharon and the others went up to the third floor. He visited Sharon's room while she took a blue raincoat from the closet and a slim umbrella, also blue. Then she came to his room while he put on an English mackintosh and a hat of Irish tweed. Out in the corridor they met their companions, variously raincoated, and went down to the lobby again. Pitt waited for them there. His face was solemn.

"Who'd have thought a meeting like this would bring on such happenings?" he said.

"I would, for one," replied Manco at once. He wore a

THE SCHOOL OF DARKNESS 169

poncho over his beaded shirt with his braids hanging upon it, and a wide-brimmed black hat on his head.

"That strange death of Exum Layton saddens me," said Pitt. "It saddens you, too, doesn't it? He didn't have to die like that."

"He had to die like that if some enemy managed it," said Father Bundren.

"You don't think it was a natural death," Pitt almost accused.

"I think it was a highly unnatural death," said Father Bundren. "I think it was murder, though we may not be able to prove it. Not just yet."

They went together to the outer door, and into the open air that was as heavy as a smothering cloak.

Night had fallen. Overhead, the sky was fairly swaddled with clouds. No sign of that bright moon, those spangles of stars, that had been so evident the night before. As they stood together for a moment, a great red flash of lightning crawled above, like a wriggling snake. Then thunder rolled, as loud and long as a massed ruffle of drums. Sharon clutched Thunstone's arm, held it close against her body.

"Let's go, then," said Pitt.

He led the way. Behind him walked Shimada and Kyoki. Then came Thunstone and Sharon, and at the rear Father Bundren and Manco. The streetlight at the crossing seemed caught up in a sort of filthy fog. They crossed the pavement and entered the campus. They could barely make out the buildings in the murk.

They passed a heavy-trunked tree, an oak. Thunstone had barely noticed it before. But now it was evident; it almost leaned at them. In its rough bark seemed to be set a face, with deep, staring eyes and a gash of mouth below them. It stared, and Thunstone stared back as he walked by.

Another glare of lighting, which for a moment lighted their way luridly. And then the accompanying thunder,

170   THE SCHOOL OF DARKNESS

louder than a drum now, loud as the explosion of a bomb. A snuffling wind had begun to rise. Sharon caught her breath, she clung to Thunstone's arm.

They came to where lights showed the entrance to the auditorium. People were streaming in, despite the threat of the storm. As Pitt led the way up the steps, rain came down abruptly, streams and splashes of rain, and again lightning and thunder as they went in. The tempest strove loudly against the roof of the auditorium.

XV

As they paused in the lobby, the massive building seemed to tremble, like a ship on a high sea. Lee Pitt looked around at them, his face very sober.

"I'd suggest that you others go ahead if you want to be backstage," he said. "I haven't asked why you're doing that, but I figure it's all right. Go ahead."

Father Bundren and Manco went down the aisle, Sharon close behind them, then Shimada and Kyoki. Pitt stood with Thunstone. He nodded to a dripping couple, probably man and wife, who came in and entered the auditorium. Finally he said, "Now we'll go down together."

The carpeted floor of the aisle seemed to tremble under Thunstone's feet. The vaulted roof overhead rasped and rattled as though the rain would tear it open. People along the aisle seats spoke to Pitt, and several spoke to Thunstone. Almost in the front row sat Rowley Thorne wrapped in something black, and Grizel Fian in the red dress she liked so much. Thunstone paused beside them.

"Good evening," he said. "Your orchestra outside is in good tune."

Thorne glowered, red-eyed. "You were warned not to come and speak here tonight."

"I know," said Thunstone. "But here I am, I'm going to speak, and these people can hear me."

He and Pitt headed for the entrance to the stage. The others were grouped there. Manco smoked his elephant

172 THE SCHOOL OF DARKNESS

pipe, and Shimada and Kyoki watched the curl of vapor rise from it.

"I don't know what you people intend to do, but I'll hang around out here and see," said Pitt. "Where do you want to wait and listen?"

"Back of the dark hangings," said Father Bundren. "Professor Shimada and his young friend there at the far side, where the entry is. The countess and I will be upstage, where there's a way to come on if we need to. And Chief Manco here."

"All right, and when I've introduced Mr. Thunstone I'll come back and stand here with Chief Manco. It's about eight o'clock now. Are you ready?"

"Wait." Thunstone draped his mackintosh on a chair and put his hat on it. He drew his silver blade and leaned the shank of the cane against the chair. Pitt stared but said nothing.

The houselights had dimmed; the overhead stage lights and the footlights had come up. Pitt walked onstage and to the lectern. Thunstone straightened his necktie and followed at his side. He carried his drawn blade. Pitt faced the audience, which ceased its usual patter of conversation. Rain poured outside.

"Ladies and gentlemen," said Pitt, "a great many of you have braved a considerable spell of ugly weather to come here tonight. You have come to where you can hear Mr. John Thunstone. I need not remind you further of his distinguished career as an explorer of strange occurrences, sometimes chancy occurrences. It wouldn't be proper of me to name these matters over to you. There are too many of them. Let me only introduce you to Mr. Thunstone himself."

He walked off swiftly. Thunstone came to the lectern and laid his blade across it and bracketed his big hands upon it. He looked down at Thorne and Grizel Fian, and saw the

THE SCHOOL OF DARKNESS

173

glitter of their eyes as they looked back at him. A great crash of thunder sounded outside, and the lights above him dimmed for a moment, then came on again.

"Good evening," he said into the microphone. "I'm here to say some specific things, and to say that I've been told not to talk here at all. I was told that in threatening terms, but I'm not taking any such orders tonight. I'm going to make statements, and some of those statements will be accusations."

Something like a groan of derision rose among the listeners. No doubt but that he had enemies there. Peering, he could spot the bearded giant he had met in the cemetery, he saw the red-haired girl, and plainly he could see Thorne and Grizel Fian, sitting forward and glaring.

"Let's briefly consider devil worship as part of our American history and culture," Thunstone said. "In colonial times it was everywhere, not just in Salem. The first to be hanged for a witch in New England went to the gallows almost half a century before the Salem trials. There were accusations and frequent executions among people of all social classes, in New York, Virginia, Pennsylvania, Michigan, everywhere. Laws against witchcraft were rescinded, but charges were made up to the very time of the Revolution and beyond. Today the worshipers of devils, the dealers in black magic, aren't brought into court for their performances and claims. They advertise themselves, they attend their meetings without fear or concealment. In the 1940s groups of conjurors were photographed as they tried, by magic, to kill Adolf Hitler. Maybe they couldn't. By some reports, Hilter himself was caught up in pagan rites. It took invading Russian armies to drive him to suicide."

Everyone was listening.

"Here and there today we have thriving colleges of witchcraft, very frank and public in offering their beliefs and instructions. In California we have the so-called Church of

174 THE SCHOOL OF DARKNESS

Satan, complete with a highly picturesque pope and branch establishments throughout the United States and overseas in Europe. In England there is another Black Church of the same sort that claims more than a hundred covens of members. And I repeat what you heard, earlier today, from Professor Tashiro Shimada—these beliefs are balefully active here in your town of Buford, where their followers hope to make use of Buford State University, make here a school of darkness."

Loud thunder then. The lights dimmed but did not quite go out, then shone again. The auditorium quivered; the floor under Thunstone's feet seemed to tilt for a moment.

"Am I recognized?" asked Thunstone. "Is all this attention directed at me? I don't know if I should feel worthy. As it says in *Tom Sawyer,* why this massed artillery bombardment to destroy one bug? Maybe I'm to be frightened into silence, into retreat. I promise you, I won't be frightened into either."

"Bawww!" rose a voice in the audience, like the bellow of a bull.

"And barnyard imitations won't stampede me," said Thunstone. "And at least, that furious storm outside will discourage any protesting souls from going out into it. I've promised you some information on the devil's disciples in Buford, and the information I'll give is firsthand."

"Liar!" screamed someone. It may have been Grizel Fian.

"No, I'm a truth teller and a truth seeker," said Thunstone. "It's been my life's work to seek the nature of reality. Even when that nature seems to be beyond nature, beyond the nature we know and recognize. Here goes."

Several voices in the auditorium seemed to be humming, crooning. It might have been a song, and not a pleasant song.

"The founding of the college that has become this Buford State University partakes of the supernormal," pursued

THE SCHOOL OF DARKNESS 175

Thunstone. "I've heard only semilegendary reports of the early days of enchantment here, and of how they got support, financial backing, at the time the college was founded. As I say, I've only heard those things, and maybe you'll object to hearsay evidence. But I've witnessed a ceremony, and a baleful one, myself. It happened in the basement of Grizel Fian's house."

"That's another of your lies!" This time it was manifestly Grizel Fian who shouted the accusation.

"No, ma'am, it's another of my truths," Thunstone fairly snapped back at her. "The truth hurts you, doesn't it? You know that I was there. You know that you and your followers tried to put a deadly curse on me, and that it didn't work. I watched what you tried with an effigy and an enchanted spear. I broke up your meeting, and there was nothing you could do about that."

Here and there in the gathering, people began to hoot and howl. Plainly Thorne and Grizel Fian had brought a considerable group with them.

Mighty thunder again, and the lights went out above Thunstone's head. At the same moment, other lights blinked into view, glowing red points. They were like embers. They revealed the faces of those who bore them, tense, distorted faces. The faces turned up and glared at Thunstone.

"Thanks for that illumination," Thunstone said, raising his voice to be heard. "It's to light a way to destruction, isn't it? Whose destruction?"

The overhead lights came up; the microphone would be working again. Thunstone said into it, "Today we had a cowardly murder on campus. Some of you know the student who died, Exum Layton."

The whole stage seemed to sway and tremble under Thunstone's feet. This must be how the bridge of a ship was to a captain in a typhoon, he thought, and the captain might

176 THE SCHOOL OF DARKNESS

go down with his ship. But this ship would not go down, and he, Thunstone, would not go down either.

"You don't want to hear me, but you will!" shouted Thunstone at the top of his lungs. "Exum Layton gave up his part in devil worship here, and he died. Coincidence? They're trying to find out, by conducting an autopsy. But I've already found out, and I say to you, it was murder by black magic!"

Thorne had risen in his seat. "You're through, Thunstone!" he yelled. "You're through!"

"Yes!" cried others. "Yes!"

Thunstone grinned down at Thorne, every tooth bared. "No," he called back. "I'm not finished, I've just begun. And do you want to try it on with me again? Why not come up on stage with me? Do you dare?"

A moment of utter silence except for the storm, while the lights dimmed and grew strong again. The voice of Rowley Thorne rose:

"The time is not yet. Go on, talk. It will be your last statement."

"Did you hear that?" cried Thunstone into the microphone. "Rowley Thorne threatens me with death. I subpoena everyone here tonight as witnesses to that." Again he looked down at Thorne. "If you can kill me, and I don't think you can, you're guilty of malice aforethought."

"I didn't say kill you," came back Thorne. "I'll just exile you into silence."

A wild yell went up, from many throats. The coals of fire stirred, whirled, in the hands of Thorne's supporters. Others in the audience sat motionless, rapt, stunned.

"You know what I mean," Thorne blared.

"Try it," said Thunstone.

"Here I come!"

Thorne came up out of his seat. Nearby red glimmers showed that he was swathed in a black cape, folded up to

THE SCHOOL OF DARKNESS 177

his bull throat. He ran to the rail of the orchestra pit and seemed to float to the stage. With him came Grizel Fian in the red dress she liked to wear. How they made that jump puzzled Thunstone. Something must have lifted them, floated them, made them fly.

Thorne came to stage center, almost next to where Thunstone stood at the lectern. He raised his arms on high, flinging the black cape from his body. Underneath it he was dressed in a black suit and a black vest which came to his plowshare chin.

"Listen to what is true, what is great!" he bellowed at the audience. "I'm here to tell you and to put this man Thunstone to shame!"

"Hear the truth!" shrilled Grizel Fian. Her eyes stared, her bosom heaved and rolled like billows at sea. "We bring you the truth, hear it while you have the chance!"

The audience sat transfixed. The floor pitched. Overhead, the rain rushed down on the roof.

"You dare face me," said Thunstone, turning from the lectern toward Thorne so close to him. "You're a slow learner, aren't you? How many times—"

"The last battle decides the war," Thorne mouthed. His eyes looked bright red, as though full of blood. "I've learned what to do, and now I'll do it."

The bearers of the red coals had come forward along the aisles, were massed at the rail of the orchestra pit. Others, the people who had only come to hear, weaved where they sat. Several had risen in the aisles, as though to run away.

"You can win only against the helpless," Thunstone said to Thorne and to Grizel Fian. "Helpless victims, like Exum Layton. I've come prepared."

"You have nothing! Nothing!" Grizel Fian spewed at him.

"You'll depart into nothingness," crooned Thorne, showing his blocky teeth. "I'll put you there."

178 THE SCHOOL OF DARKNESS

"Do you remember when you tried it before?" Thunstone jibed at him. "Tried it before, and who was it went into nothingness? Try it now."

"Ooooh!" the fire bearers at the orchestra rail moaned in chorus.

"Now my wish, my prayer will come true!" Rowley Thorne shouted. "Hear me, Moloch, Lucifer, Pemoath."

"Anector, Somiator, sleep ye not," said Grizel Fian, as though it were an antistrophe.

"I've heard those names," said Thunstone, quite calmly. "They don't frighten me at all. Say some more."

Again Thorne waved his huge hands. "Eko, eko, Azarak!" he bugled. "Eko, eko, Aamalek! Eko, eko, eko, eko!"

"Gibberish," pronounced Thunstone. But as he spoke, the air thickened and oppressed. It smelled like raw hides.

"Awake, strong Holaha," Thorne was chanting again. "Powerful Eabon, mighty Athe, Sada, Eroyhe—by your names, by names not to be spoken, I deliver this scoffer into your nothingness!"

With that, he hurled himself upon Thunstone.

They grappled. Thorne was strong; Thunstone knew that from other encounters. Thorne groped for Thunstone's throat, but Thunstone caught him by his heavy biceps and jammed his thumbs into the insides of the muscles, seeking and finding nerves there. He dug with all his strength. He heard Thorne howl with pain. They wrestled each other across the floor.

"No!" roared another voice. "No!"

That was Reuben Manco. He had rushed out upon the stage. So had Father Bundren, holding a crucifix on high. Shimada and Kyoki were there, talking in Japanese, and Sharon, too. Thorne tried to hook a foot back of Thunstone's heel to throw him, but Thunstone stepped clear of

THE SCHOOL OF DARKNESS   179

the entanglement and, with all his strength, heaved Thorne
up above his head. Grizel Fian shrieked.

Then a silvery jangle of sound. Sharon was ringing the
bell Thunstone had given her. Thunstone threw Thorne
from him.

That was all. Thorne winked out of sight in midair. Grizel Fian had vanished, too. They were gone.

At the same instant, the rain and the wind stopped. There
was silence all through the hall. Thunstone saw the bearers
of the red lights scrambling off along the aisles, in headlong
flight for the open.

He returned to the lectern. He smiled out at those who
had stayed. Then he turned to where Sharon stood trembling, the bell still in her hand.

"You did what was needed," he told her. "They wanted
to send me away somewhere—another plane, another dimension. But the spirits they called on went back without
me, and took them along instead."

He spoke into the microphone:

"Ladies and gentlemen, don't ask me where they went. I
don't know, I have only dark suspicions."

XVI

Monday noon.

They sat in Thunstone's room, where they had sat again and again in sober council. The councils were over, at least as they concerned the vanished Rowley Thorne and Grizel Fian. But all Sunday and all Monday morning had been busy, with the Buford police and men of the State Bureau of Investigation, and with newspaper interviews. All of them were heartily tired of those.

"At last I've had time to hear from the hospital and the autopsy on Exum Layton," said Thunstone. "They're calling it a cardiac arrest, but they're mystified, like everyone else. No real rupture in the region of the heart, just a stablike wound there, as though with a blade. It was something like what they tried against me and couldn't get done. The body's been released to the funeral home in town."

"And the funeral will be in the chapel there, at ten o'clock tomorrow morning," said Father Bundren. "I hope all of you will attend."

"If you permit me, I would like to provide a tombstone," said Shimada. "One such as you see all through the cemetery, and upon it, 'Exum Layton, Who Came into the Light.'"

"How splendid," said Sharon.

Manco puffed on his elephant pipe. "Those police kept asking questions, and I kept telling the truth, and they kept not believing me," he said. "They wanted someone to vouch for me, someone other than you people. At the time, proba-

THE SCHOOL OF DARKNESS 181

bly they wanted to suspect you too, but couldn't think of any good suspicions. All I could think of was to call Dr. Clark at the hospital. He vouched for me all the way, got them off my back. But I had to promise him to talk about Cherokee medicine methods to a group of med students and residents. That's for tomorrow in the afternoon, so I'll have a full Tuesday before I head home."

"Sharon and I will spend a few more days here," said Thunstone. "Rest a trifle and talk to friends we've made."

"Yes," said Sharon, cradling the silver bell in her hands. "This helped, didn't it?" she said, and held it out to Thunstone. "Don't you want it back?"

"It's a present to you," he said. "Have you had time to study the words on it? You'll find the names of Saint Cecilia and Saint Dunstan, for music and silverwork. And a motto in Latin, *Est mea terror vox daemonoirum.*"

"My voice is the terror of all demons," translated Father Bundren. "That's a powerful talisman, Countess. I'll say with Thunstone that when you rang it, it had its effect."

"Where did they go?" asked Shimada. "Thorne and Grizel Fian—where?"

"They softly and suddenly vanished away, like the man in 'The Hunting of the Snark.' "

"I can't do anything but theorize," said Thunstone. "They were trying to send me away—to another plane, another dimension, another existence. Maybe to limbo. Thorne went there once before when he tried to send me there and failed. Grizel Fian somehow charmed him back into this world we know. Now she's gone with him. I don't know where they are, or how long they'll stay."

"*Wagh,*" said Manco. "Forever, I hope."

"Amen to that," said Father Bundren. "Others have left Buford, the police tell me. Students, townspeople, even one faculty member, all in a hurry. I'd suggest that, here in Buford, their room is better than their company."

182   THE SCHOOL OF DARKNESS

Thunstone rose. "Shouldn't we go and have some lunch?"

They went down to the dining room and found a table. The young waiter who had served them on Saturday night brought menus.

"Mr. Thunstone, I looked for you yesterday," he said, mildly reproachful. "You promised me your autograph."

"I was busy all yesterday, didn't get anything to eat but sandwiches," said Thunstone.

Manco studied the waiter. "You weren't one of that crowd that cleared out of here without barely stopping to pack," he said.

"That crazy devil crowd?" said the waiter. "I never paid them any heed. I don't believe in their talk."

"Don't you?" said Thunstone. "Well, give me some paper and I'll autograph to you personally. What's your name, son?"